P. G. Wodehouse was born in Guildford in 1881 and educated at Dulwich College. After working for the Hong Kong and Shanghai Bank for two years, he left to earn his living as a journalist and storywriter, writing the 'By the Way' column in the old *Globe*. He also contributed a series of school stories to a magazine for boys, the *Captain*, in one of which Psmith made his first appearance. Going to America before the First World War, he sold a serial to the *Saturday Evening Post*, and for the next twenty-five years almost all his books appeared first in this magazine. He was part author and writer of the lyrics of eighteen musical comedies including *Kissing Time*. He married in 1914 and in 1955 took American citizenship. He wrote over ninety books, and his work has won world-wide acclaim, having been translated into many languages. *The Times* hailed him as a 'comic genius recognized in his lifetime as a classic and an old master of farce'.

P. G. Wodehouse said, 'I believe there are two ways of writing novels. One is mine, making a sort of musical comedy without music and ignoring real life altogether; the other is going right deep down into life and not caring a damn . . .' He was created a Knight of the British Empire in the New Year's Honours List in 1975. In a BBC interview he said that he had no ambition left now that he had been knighted and there was a waxwork of him in Madame Tussaud's. He died on St Valentine's Day in 1975 at the age of ninety-three.

MIKE AND PSMITH

P. G. WODEHOUSE

PENGUIN BOOKS

PENGUIN BOOKS

Published by the Penguin Group
Penguin Books Ltd, 27 Wrights Lane, London W8 5TZ, England
Penguin Putnam Inc., 375 Hudson Street, New York, New York 10014, USA
Penguin Books Australia Ltd, Ringwood, Victoria, Australia
Penguin Books Canada Ltd, 10 Alcorn Avenue, Toronto, Ontario, Canada M4V 3B2
Penguin Books (NZ) Ltd, Private Bag 102902, NSMC, Auckland, New Zealand

Penguin Books Ltd, Registered Offices: Harmondsworth, Middlesex, England

First published as *Mike* by A. & C. Black 1909
Revised edition published in two parts as *Mike at Wrykyn* and *Mike and Psmith*
by Herbert Jenkins 1953
Mike and Psmith published in Penguin Books 1990
7 9 10 8

Copyright 1909, 1953 by P. G. Wodehouse
All rights reserved

Filmset in Garamond
Printed in England by Clays Ltd, St Ives plc

CONTENTS

CONTENTS

CHAPTER I

MR. JACKSON MAKES UP HIS MIND

IF Mike had been in time for breakfast that fatal Easter morning he might have gathered from the expression on his father's face, as Mr. Jackson opened the envelope containing his school report and read the contents, that the document in question was not exactly a pæan of praise from beginning to end. But he was late, as usual. Mike always was late for breakfast in the holidays.

When he came down on this particular morning, the meal was nearly over. Mr. Jackson had disappeared, taking his correspondence with him; Mrs. Jackson had gone into the kitchen, and when Mike appeared the thing had resolved itself into a mere vulgar brawl between Phyllis and Ella for the jam, while Marjory, recently affecting a grown-up air, looked on in a detached sort of way, as if these juvenile gambols distressed her.

"Hullo, Mike," she said, jumping up as he entered; "here you are—I've been keeping everything hot for you."

"Have you? Thanks awfully. I say——" his eye wandered in mild surprise round the table. "I'm a bit late."

Marjory was bustling about, fetching and carrying for Mike, as she always did. She had adopted him at an early age, and did the thing thoroughly. She was fond of her other brothers, especially when they made centuries in first-class cricket, but Mike was her favourite. She would field out in the deep as a natural thing when Mike was batting at the net in the paddock, though for the others, even for Joe, who had played in all five Test Matches in the previous summer, she would do it only as a favour.

7

Phyllis and Ella finished their dispute and went out. Marjory sat on the table and watched Mike eat.

"Your report came this morning, Mike," she said.

The kidneys failed to retain Mike's undivided attention. He looked up interested. "What did it say?"

"I didn't see—I only caught sight of the Wrykyn crest on the envelope. Father didn't say anything."

Mike seemed concerned. "I say, that looks rather rotten! I wonder if it was awfully bad. It's the first I've had from Appleby."

"It can't be any worse than the horrid ones Mr. Blake used to write when you were in his form."

"No, that's a comfort," said Mike philosophically. "Think there's any more tea in that pot?"

"I call it a shame," said Marjory: "they ought to be jolly glad to have you at Wrykyn just for cricket, instead of writing beastly reports that make father angry and don't do any good to anybody."

"Last Christmas he said he'd take me away if I got another one."

"He didn't mean it really, I *know* he didn't! He couldn't! You're the best bat Wrykyn's ever had."

"What ho!" interpolated Mike.

"You *are*. Everybody says you are. Why, you got your first the very first term you were there—even Joe didn't do anything nearly so good as that. Saunders says you're simply bound to play for England in another year or two."

"Saunders is a jolly good chap. He bowled me a half-volley on the off the first ball I had in a school match. By the way, I wonder if he's out at the net now. Let's go and see."

Saunders the professional was setting up the net when they arrived. Mike put on his pads and went to the wicket, while Marjory and the dogs retired as usual to the far hedge to retrieve.

She was kept busy. Saunders was a good sound bowler of the M.C.C. minor match type, and there had been a time

8

when he had worried Mike considerably, but Mike had been in the Wrykyn team for three seasons now, and each season he had advanced tremendously in his batting. He had filled out in three years. He had always had the style, and now he had the strength as well, Saunder's bowling on a true wicket seemed simple to him. It was early in the Easter holidays, but already he was beginning to find his form. Saunders, who looked on Mike as his own special invention, was delighted.

"If you don't be worried by being too anxious now that you're captain, Master Mike," he said, "you'll make a century every match next term."

"I wish I wasn't; it's a beastly responsibility."

Henfrey, the Wrykyn cricket captain of the previous season, was not returning next term, and Mike was to reign in his stead. He liked the prospect, but it certainly carried with it a rather awe-inspiring responsibility. At night sometimes he would lie awake, appalled by the fear of losing his form, or making a hash of things by choosing the wrong men to play for the school and leaving the right men out. It is no light thing to captain a public school at cricket.

As he was walking towards the house, Phyllis met him. "Oh, I've been hunting for you, Mike; father wants you."

"What for?"

"I don't know."

"Where?"

"He's in the study. He seems——" added Phyllis, throwing in the information by way of a make-weight, "in a beastly temper."

Mike's jaw fell slightly. "I hope the dickens it's nothing to do with that bally report," was his muttered exclamation.

Mike's dealings with his father were as a rule of a most pleasant nature. Mr. Jackson was an understanding sort of man, who treated his sons as companions. From time to time, however, breezes were apt to ruffle the placid sea of good-fellowship. Mike's end-of-term report was an unfailing wind-raiser; indeed, on the arrival of Mr. Blake's sarcastic *résumé* of Mike's shortcomings at the end of the previous term, there had been something not unlike a typhoon. It was on this occasion that Mr. Jackson had solemnly declared his intention of removing Mike from Wrykyn unless the critics became more flattering; and Mr. Jackson was a man of his word.

It was with a certain amount of apprehension, therefore, that Jackson entered the study.

"Come in, Mike," said his father, kicking the waste-paper basket; "I want to speak to you."

Mike, skilled in omens, scented a row in the offing. Only in moments of emotion was Mr. Jackson in the habit of booting the basket.

There followed an awkward silence, which Mike broke by remarking that he had carted a half-volley from Saunders over the on-side hedge that morning.

"It was just a bit short and off the leg stump, so I stepped out—may I bag the paper-knife for a jiffy? I'll just show——"

"Never mind about cricket now," said Mr. Jackson; "I want you to listen to this report."

"Oh, is that my report, father?" said Mike, with a sort of sickly interest, much as a dog about to be washed might evince in his tub.

"It is," replied Mr. Jackson in measured tones, "your report; what is more, it is without exception the worst report you have ever had."

"Oh, I say!" groaned the record-breaker.

"'His conduct,'" quoted Mr. Jackson, "'has been unsatisfactory in the extreme, both in and out of school.'"

"It wasn't anything really. I only happened——"

Remembering suddenly that what he had happened to do was to drop a cannon-ball (the school weight) on the form-room floor, not once, but on several occasions, he paused.

"'French bad; conduct disgraceful——'"

"Everybody rags in French."

"'Mathematics bad. Inattentive and idle.'"

"Nobody does much work in Maths."

"'Latin poor. Greek, very poor.'"

"We were doing Thucydides, Book Two, last term— all speeches and doubtful readings, and cruxes and things— beastly hard! Everybody says so."

"Here are Mr. Appleby's remarks: 'The boy has genuine ability, which he declines to use in the smallest degree.'"

Mike moaned a moan of righteous indignation.

"'An abnormal proficiency at games has apparently destroyed all desire in him to realize the more serious issues of life.' There is more to the same effect."

Mr. Appleby was a master with very definite ideas as to what constituted a public-school master's duties. As a man he was distinctly pro-Mike. He understood cricket, and some of Mike's strokes on the off gave him thrills of pure æsthetic joy; but as a master he always made it his habit to regard the manners and customs of the boys in his form with an unbiased eye, and to an unbiased eye Mike in a form-room was about as near the extreme edge as a boy could be, and Mr. Appleby said as much in a clear firm hand.

"You remember what I said to you about your report at Christmas, Mike?" said Mr. Jackson, folding the lethal document and replacing it in its envelope.

Mike said nothing; there was a sinking feeling in his interior.

"I shall abide by what I said."

Mike's heart thumped.

"You will not go back to Wrykyn next term."

Somewhere in the world the sun was shining, birds were twittering; somewhere in the world, lambkins frisked and peasants sang blithely at their toil (flat, perhaps, but still blithely), but to Mike at that moment the sky was black, and an icy wind blew over the face of the earth.

The tragedy had happened, and there was an end of it. He made no attempt to appeal against the sentence. He knew it would be useless, his father when he made up his mind, having all the unbending tenacity of the normally easygoing man.

Mr. Jackson was sorry for Mike. He understood him, and for that reason he said very little now.

"I am sending you to Sedleigh," was his next remark.

Sedleigh! Mike sat up with a jerk. He knew Sedleigh by name—one of those schools with about a hundred boys which you never hear of except when they send up their gym team to Aldershot, or their Eight to Bisley. Mike's outlook on life was that of a cricketer, pure and simple. What had Sedleigh ever done? What were they ever likely to do? Whom did they play? What Old Sedleighan had ever done anything at cricket? Perhaps they didn't even *play* cricket!

"But it's an awful hole," he said blankly.

Mr. Jackson could read Mike's mind like a book. Mike's point of view was plain to him. He did not approve of it, but he knew that in Mike's place and at Mike's age he would have felt the same. He spoke dryly to hide his sympathy.

"It is not a large school," he said, "and I don't suppose it could play Wrykyn at cricket, but it has one merit—boys work there. Young Barlitt won a Balliol scholarship from Sedleigh last year." Barlitt was the vicar's son, a silent, spectacled youth who did not enter very largely into Mike's world. They had met occasionally at tennis-parties, but not much conversation had ensued. Barlitt's mind was massive, but his topics of conversation were not Mike's.

"Mr. Barlitt speaks very highly of Sedleigh," added Mr. Jackson.

Mike said nothing, which was a good deal better than saying what he would have liked to have said.

CHAPTER II

SEDLEIGH

THE train, which had been stopping everywhere for the last half-hour, pulled up again, and Mike, seeing the name of the station, got up, opened the door, and hurled a bag out on to the platform in an emphatic and vindictive manner. Then he got out himself and looked about him.

"For the school, sir?" inquired the solitary porter, bustling up, as if he hoped by sheer energy to deceive the traveller into thinking that Sedleigh station was staffed by a great army of porters.

Mike nodded. A sombre nod. The nod Napoleon might have given if somebody had met him in 1812, and said, " So you're back from Moscow, eh?" Mike was feeling thoroughly jaundiced. The future seemed wholly gloomy. And, so far from attempting to make the best of things, he had set himself deliberately to look on the dark side. He thought, for instance, that he had never seen a more repulsive porter, or one more obviously incompetent than the man who had attached himself with a firm grasp to the handle of the bag as he strode off in the direction of the luggage-van. He disliked his voice, his appearance, and the colour of his hair. Also the boots he wore. He hated the station, and the man who took his ticket.

"Young gents at the school, sir," said the porter, perceiving from Mike's *distrait* air that the boy was a stranger to the place, "goes up in the bus mostly. It's waiting here, sir. Hi, George!"

"I'll walk, thanks," said Mike frigidly.

"It's a goodish step, sir."

"Here you are."

"Thank you, sir. I'll send up your luggage by the bus, sir. Which 'ouse was it you was going to?"

"Outwood's."

"Right, sir. It's straight on up this road to the school. You can't miss it, sir."

"Worse luck," said Mike.

He walked off up the road, sorrier for himself than ever. It was such absolutely rotten luck. About now, instead of being on his way to a place where they probably ran a halma team instead of a cricket eleven, and played hunt-the-slipper in winter, he would be on the point of arriving at Wrykyn. And as captain of cricket, at that. Which was the bitter part of it. He had never been in command. For the last two seasons he had been the star man, going in first, and heading the averages easily at the end of the season; and the three captains under whom he had played during his career as a Wrykynian, Burgess, Enderby, and Henfrey, had always been sportsmen to him. But it was not the same thing. He had meant to do such a lot for Wrykyn cricket this term. He had had an entirely new system of coaching in his mind. Now it might never be used. He had handed it on in a letter to Strachan, who would be captain in his place; but probably Strachan would have some scheme of his own. There is nobody who could not edit a paper in the ideal way; and there is nobody who has not a theory of his own about cricket-coaching at school.

Wrykyn, too, would be weak this year, now that he was no longer there. Strachan was a good, free bat on his day, and, if he survived a few overs, might make a century in an hour, but he was not to be depended upon. There was no doubt that Mike's sudden withdrawal meant that Wrykyn would have a bad time that season. And it had been such a wretched athletic year for the school. The football fifteen been hopeless, and had lost both the Ripton matches, the return by over sixty points. Sheen's victory in the light-weights at Aldershot had been their one success. And now, on top of all this, the captain of cricket was removed during the Easter holidays. Mike's heart bled for Wrykyn, and he found himself loathing Sedleigh and all its works with a great loathing.

The only thing he could find in its favour was the fact that it was set in a very pretty country. Of a different type from the Wrykyn country, but almost as good. For three miles Mike made his way through woods and past fields. Once he crossed a river. It was soon after this that he caught sight, from the top of a hill, of a group of buildings that wore an unmistakably school-like look.

This must be Sedleigh.

Ten minutes' walk brought him to the school gates, and a baker's boy directed him to Mr. Outwood's.

There were three houses in a row, separated from the school buildings by a cricket-field. Outwood's was the middle one of these.

Mike went to the front door, and knocked. At Wrykyn he had always charged in at the beginning of term at the boys' entrance, but this formal reporting of himself at Sedleigh suited his mood.

He inquired for Mr. Outwood, and was shown into a room lined with books. Presently the door opened, and the house-master appeared.

There was something pleasant and homely about Mr. Outwood. In appearance he reminded Mike of Smee in "Peter Pan." He had the same eyebrows and pince-nez and the same motherly look.

" Jackson?" he said mildly.

"Yes, sir."

"I am very glad to see you, very glad indeed. Perhaps you would like a cup of tea after your journey. I think you might like a cup of tea. You come from Crofton, in Shropshire, I understand, Jackson, near Brindleford? It is a part of the country which I have always wished to visit. I dare say you have frequently seen the Cluniac Priory of St. Ambrose at Brindleford?"

Mike, who would not have recognized a Cluniac Priory if you had handed him one on a tray, said he had not.

"Dear me! You have missed an opportunity which I should have been glad to have. I am preparing a book on Ruined Abbeys and Priories of England, and it has always been my wish to see the Cluniac Priory of St. Ambrose. A deeply interesting relic of the sixteenth century. Bishop Geofffrey 1133-40——"

"Shall I go across to the boys' part, sir?"

"What? Yes. Oh, yes. Quite so. And perhaps you would like a cup of tea after your journey? No? Quite so. Quite so. You should make a point of visiting the remains of the Cluniac Priory in the summer holidays, Jackson. You will find the matron in her room. In many respects it is unique. The northern altar is in a state of really wonderful preservation. It consists of a solid block of masonry five feet long and two and a half wide, with chamfered plinth, standing quite free from the apse wall. It will well repay a visit. Good-bye for the present, Jackson, good-bye."

Mike wandered across to the other side of the house, his gloom visibly deepened. All alone in a strange school, where they probably played hop-scotch, with a house-master who offered one cups of tea after one's journey and talked about chamfered plinths and apses. It was a little hard.

He strayed about, finding his bearings, and finally came to a room which he took to be the equivalent of the senior day-room at a Wrykyn house. Everywhere else he had found nothing but emptiness. Evidently he had come by an earlier train than was usual. But this room was occupied.

A very long, thin youth, with a solemn face and immaculate clothes, was leaning against the mantelpiece. As Mike entered, he fumbled in his top left waistcoat pocket, produced an eyeglass attached to a cord, and fixed it in his right eye. With the help of this aid to vision he inspected Mike in silence for a while, then, having flicked an invisible speck of dust from the left sleeve of his coat, he spoke.

"Hullo," he said.

He spoke in a tired voice.

16

"Hullo," said Mike.

"Take a seat," said the immaculate one. "If you don't mind dirtying your bags, that's to say. Personally, I don't see any prospect of ever sitting down in this place. It looks to me as if they meant to use these chairs as mustard-and-cress beds. A Nursery Garden in the Home. That sort of idea. My name," he added pensively, "is Smith. What's yours?"

CHAPTER III

PSMITH

"JACKSON," said Mike.

"Are you the Bully, the Pride of the School, or the Boy who is Led Astray and takes to Drink in Chapter Sixteen?"

"The last, for choice," said Mike, "but I've only just arrived, so I don't know."

"The boy—what will he become? Are you new here, too, then?"

"Yes! Why, are you new?"

"Do I look as if I belonged here? I'm the latest import. Sit down on yonder settee, and I will tell you the painful story of my life. By the way, before I start, there's just one thing. If you ever have occasion to write to me, would you mind sticking a P at the beginning of my name? P-s-m-i-t-h See? There are too many Smiths, and I don't care for Smythe. My father's content to worry along in the old-fashioned way, but I've decided to strike out a fresh line. I shall found a new dynasty. The resolve came to me unexpectedly this morning. I jotted it down on the back of an envelope. In conversation you may address me as Rupert (though I hope you won't), or simply Smith, the P not being sounded. Cp. the name Zbysco, in which the Z is given a similar miss-in-baulk. See?"

Mike said he saw. Psmith thanked him with a certain stately old-world courtesy.

"Let us start at the beginning," he resumed. "My infancy. When I was but a babe, my eldest sister was bribed with a shilling an hour by my nurse to keep an eye on me, and see that I did not raise Cain. At the end of the first day she struck for one-and-six, and got it. We now pass to my boyhood. At an early age, I was sent to Eton, everybody predicting a bright career for me. But," said Psmith solemnly, fixing an owl-like gaze on Mike through the eyeglass, "it was not to be."

"No?" said Mike.

"No. I was superannuated last term."

"Bad luck."

"For Eton, yes. But what Eton loses, Sedleigh gains."

"But why Sedleigh, of all places?"

"This is the most painful part of my narrative. It seems that a certain scug in the next village to ours happened last year to collar a Balliol——"

"Not Barlitt!" exclaimed Mike.

"That was the man. The son of the vicar. The vicar told the curate, who told our curate, who told our vicar, who told my father, who sent me off here to get a Balliol too. Do *you* know Barlitt?"

"His father's vicar of our village. It was because his son got a Balliol that I was sent here."

"Do you come from Crofton?"

"Yes."

"I've lived at Lower Benford all my life. We are practically long-lost brothers. Cheer a little, will you?"

Mike felt as Robinson Crusoe felt when he met Friday. Here was a fellow human being in this desert place. He could almost have embraced Psmith. The very sound of the name Lower Benford was heartening. His dislike for his new school was not diminished, but now he felt that life there might at least be tolerable.

"Where were you before you came here?" asked Psmith. "You have heard my painful story. Now tell me yours."

"Wrykyn. My father took me away because I got such a lot of bad reports."

"My reports from Eton were simply scurrilous. There's a libel action in every sentence. How do you like this place from what you've seen of it?"

"Rotten."

"I am with you, Comrade Jackson. You won't mind my calling you Comrade, will you? I've just become a Socialist. It's a great scheme. You ought to be one. You work for the equal distribution of property, and start by collaring all you can and sitting on it. We must stick together. We are companions in misfortune. Lost lambs. Sheep that have gone astray. Divided, we fall, together we may worry through. Have you seen Professor Radium yet? I should say Mr. Outwood. What do you think of him?"

"He doesn't seem a bad sort of chap. Bit off his nut. Jawed about apses and things."

"And thereby," said Psmith, "hangs a tale. I've been making inquiries of a stout sportsman in a sort of Salvation Army uniform, whom I met in the grounds—he's the school sergeant or something, quite a solid man—and I hear that Comrade Outwood's an archæological cove. Goes about the country beating up old ruins and fossils and things. There's an Archæological Society in the school, run by him. It goes out on half-holidays, prowling about, and is allowed to break bounds and generally steep itself to the eyebrows in reckless devilry. And, mark you, laddie, if you belong to the Archæological Society you get off cricket. To get off cricket," said Psmith, dusting his right trouser-leg, "was the dream of my youth and the aspiration of my riper years. A noble game, but a bit too thick for me. At Eton I used to have to field out at the nets till the soles of my boots wore through. I suppose you are a blood at the game? Play for the school against Loamshire, and so on."

"I'm not going to play here, at any rate," said Mike.

He had made up his mind on this point in the train. There is a certain fascination about making the very worst of a bad job. Achilles knew his business when he sat in his tent. The determination not to play cricket for Sedleigh as he could not play for Wrykyn gave Mike a sort of pleasure. To stand by with folded arms and a sombre frown, as it were, was one way of treating the situation, and one not without its meed of comfort.

Psmith approved the resolve.

"Stout fellow," he said. "'Tis well. You and I, hand in hand, will search the countryside for ruined abbeys. We will snare the elusive fossil together. Above all, we will go out of bounds. We shall thus improve our minds, and have a jolly good time as well. I shouldn't wonder if one mightn't borrow a gun from some friendly native, and do a bit of rabbit-shooting here and there. From what I saw of Comrade Outwood during our brief interview, I shouldn't think he was one of the lynx-eyed contingent. With tact we ought to be able to slip away from the merry throng of fossil-chasers, and do a bit on our own account."

"Good idea," said Mike. "We will. A chap at Wrykyn, called Wyatt, used to break out at night and shoot at cats with an air-pistol."

"It would take a lot to make me do that. I am all against anything that interferes with my sleep. But rabbits in the daytime is a scheme. We'll nose about for a gun at the earliest opp. Meanwhile we'd better go up to Comrade Outwood, and get our names shoved down for the Society."

"I vote we get some tea first somewhere."

"Then let's beat up a study. I suppose they have studies here. Let's go and look."

They went upstairs. On the first floor there was a passage with doors on either side. Psmith opened the first of these.

"This'll do us well," he said.

It was a biggish room, looking out over the school grounds. There were a couple of deal tables, two empty bookcases, and a looking-glass, hung on a nail.

"Might have been made for us," said Psmith approvingly.

"I suppose it belongs to some rotter."

"Not now."

"You aren't going to collar it!"

"That," said Psmith, looking at himself earnestly in the

mirror, and straightening his tie, "is the exact programme. We must stake out our claims. This is practical Socialism."

"But the real owner's bound to turn up some time or other."

"His misfortune, not ours. You can't expect two master-minds like us to pig it in that room downstairs. There are moments when one wants to be alone. It is imperative that we have a place to retire to after a fatiguing day. And now, if you want to be really useful, come and help me fetch up my box from down stairs. It's got a gas-ring and various things in it."

CHAPTER IV

STAKING OUT A CLAIM

Psmith, in the matter of decorating a study and preparing tea in it, was rather a critic than an executant. He was full of ideas, but he preferred to allow Mike to carry them out. It was he who suggested that the wooden bar which ran across the window was unnecessary, but it was Mike who wrenched it from its place. Similarly, it was Mike who abstracted the key from the door of the next study, though the idea was Psmith's.

"Privacy," said Psmith, as he watched Mike light the gas-ring, "is what we chiefly need in this age of publicity. If you leave a study door unlocked in these strenuous times, the first thing you know is, somebody comes right in, sits down, and begins to talk about himself. I think with a little care we ought to be able to make this room quite decently comfortable. That putrid calendar must come down, though. Do you think you could make a long arm, and haul it off the parent tin-tack? Thanks. We make progress. We make progress."

"We shall jolly well make it out of the window," said Mike, spooning up tea from a paper bag with a postcard, "if a sort of young Hackenschmidt turns up and claims the study. What are you going to do about it?"

"Don't let us worry about it. I have a presentiment that he will be an insignificant-looking little weed. How are you getting on with the evening meal?"

"Just ready. What would you give to be at Eton now? I'd give something to be at Wrykyn."

"These school reports," said Psmith sympathetically,

"are the very dickens. Many a bright young lad has been soured by them. Hullo, what's this, I wonder."

A heavy body had plunged against the door, evidently without a suspicion that there would be any resistance. A rattling of the handle followed, and a voice outside said, "Dash the door!"

"Hackenschmidt!" said Mike.

"The weed," said Psmith. "You couldn't make a long arm, could you, and turn the key? We had better give this merchant audience. Remind me later to go on with my remarks on school reports. I had several bright things to say on the subject."

Mike unlocked the door, and flung it open. Framed in the entrance was a smallish, freckled boy, wearing a pork pie hat and carrying a bag. On his face was an expression of mingled wrath and astonishment.

Psmith rose courteously from his chair, and moved forward with slow stateliness to do the honours.

"What the dickens," inquired the newcomer, "are you doing here?"

"We were having a little tea," said Psmith, "to restore our tissues after our journey. Come in and join us. We keep open house, we Psmiths. Let me introduce you to Comrade Jackson. A stout fellow. Homely in appearance, perhaps, but one of us. I am Psmith. Your own name will doubtless come up in the course of general chit-chat over the tea-cups."

"My name's Spiller, and this is my study."

Psmith leaned against the mantelpiece, put up his eyeglass, and harangued Spiller in a philosophical vein.

"Of all sad words of tongue or pen," said he, "the saddest are these: 'It might have been.' Too late! That is the bitter cry. If you had torn yourself from the bosom of the Spiller family by an earlier train, all might have been well. But no. Your father held your hand and said huskily, 'Edwin, don't leave us!' Your mother clung to you weeping, and said, 'Edwin, stay!' Your sisters——"

"I want to know what——"

24

"Your sisters froze on to your knees like little octopuses (or octopi), and screamed, 'Don't go, Edwin!' And so," said Psmith, deeply affected by his recital, "you stayed on till the later train; and, on arrival, you find strange faces in the familiar room, a people that know not Spiller." Psmith went to the table, and cheered himself with a sip of tea. Spiller's sad case had moved him greatly.

The victim of Fate seemed in no way consoled.

"It's beastly cheek, that's what I call it. Are you new chaps?"

"The very latest thing," said Psmith.

"Well, it's beastly cheek."

Mike's outlook on life was of the solid, practical order. He went straight to the root of the matter.

"What are you going to do about it?" he asked.

Spiller evaded the question.

"It's beastly cheek," he repeated. "You can't go about the place bagging studies."

"But we do," said Psmith. "In this life, Comrade Spiller, we must be prepared for every emergency. We must distinguish between the unusual and the impossible. It is unusual for people to go about the place bagging studies, so you have rashly ordered your life on the assumption that it is impossible. Error! Ah, Spiller, Spiller, let this be a lesson to you."

"Look here, I tell you what it——"

"I was in a car with a man once. I said to him: 'What would happen if you trod on that pedal thing instead of that other pedal thing?' He said, 'I couldn't. One's the foot-brake, and the other's the accelerator.' 'But suppose you did?' I said. 'I wouldn't,' he said. 'Now we'll let her rip.' So he stamped on the accelerator. Only it turned out to be the foot-brake after all, and we stopped dead, and skidded into a ditch. The advice I give to every young man starting life is: 'Never confuse the unusual and the impossible.' Take the present case. If you had only realized the possibility of somebody some day collaring your study, you might have thought out dozens of sound schemes for dealing with the matter. As it is, you are un-prepared. The thing comes on you as a surprise. The cry goes round: 'Spiller has been taken unawares. He cannot cope with the situation.'"

"Can't I! I'll——"

"What *are* you going to do about it?" said Mike.

"All I know is, I'm going to have it. It was Simpson's last term, and Simpson's left, and I'm next on the house list, so, of course, it's my study."

"But what steps," said Psmith, "are you going to take? Spiller, the man of Logic, we know. But what of Spiller, the Man of Action? How do you intend to set about it? Force is useless. I was saying to Comrade Jackson before you came in, that I didn't mind betting you were an insignificant-looking little weed. And you *are* an insignificant-looking little weed."

"We'll see what Outwood says about it."

"Not an unsound scheme. By no means a scaly project. Comrade Jackson and myself were about to interview him upon another point. We may as well all go together."

The trio made their way to the Presence, Spiller pink and determined, Mike sullen, Psmith particularly debonair. He hummed lightly as he walked, and now and then pointed out to Spiller objects of interest by the wayside.

Mr. Outwood received them with the motherly warmth which was evidently the leading characteristic of his normal manner.

"Ah, Spiller," he said. "And Smith, and Jackson. I am glad to see that you have already made friends."

"Spiller's, sir," said Psmith, laying a hand patronisingly on the study-claimer's shoulder—a proceeding violently resented by Spiller—"is a character one cannot help but respect. His nature expands before one like some beautiful flower."

Mr. Outwood received this eulogy with rather a startled expression, and gazed at the object of the tribute in a surprised way.

"Er—quite so, Smith, quite so," he said at last. "I

like to see boys in my house friendly towards one another."

"There is no vice in Spiller," pursued Psmith earnestly. "His heart is the heart of a little child."

"Please, sir," burst out this paragon of all the virtues, "I——"

"But it was not entirely with regard to Spiller that I wished to speak to you, sir, if you were not too busy."

"Not at all, Smith, not at all. Is there anything——"

"Please, sir——" began Spiller.

"I understand, sir," said Psmith, "that there is an Archæological Society in the school."

Mr. Outwood's eyes sparkled behind their pince-nez. It was a disappointment to him that so few boys seemed to wish to belong to his chosen band. Cricket and football, games that left him cold, appeared to be the main interest in their lives. It was but rarely that he could induce new boys to join. His colleague, Mr. Downing, who presided over the School Fire Brigade, never had any difficulty in finding support. Boys came readily at his call. Mr. Outwood pondered wistfully on this at times, not knowing that the Fire Brigade owed its support to the fact that it provided its light-hearted members with perfectly unparalleled opportunities for ragging, while his own band, though small, were, in the main, earnest.

"Yes, Smith," he said. "Yes. We have a small Archæological Society. I—er—in a measure look after it. Perhaps you would care to become a member?"

"Please, sir——" said Spiller.

"One moment, Spiller. Do you want to join, Smith?"

"Intensely, sir. Archæology fascinates me. A grand pursuit, sir."

"Undoubtedly, Smith. I am very pleased, very pleased indeed. I will put down your name at once."

"And Jackson's, sir."

"Jackson, too!" Mr. Outwood beamed. "I am delighted. Most delighted. This is capital. This enthusiasm is most capital."

"Spiller, sir," said Psmith sadly, "I have been unable to induce to join."

"Oh, he is one of our oldest members."

"Ah," said Psmith, tolerantly, "that accounts for it."

"Please, sir——" said Spiller.

"One moment, Spiller. We shall have the first outing of the term on Saturday. We intend to inspect the Roman Camp at Embury Hill, two miles from the school."

"We shall be there, sir."

"Capital!"

"Please, sir——" said Spiller.

"One moment, Spiller," said Psmith. "There is just one other matter, if you could spare the time, sir."

"Certainly, Smith. What is that?"

"Would there be any objection to Jackson and myself taking Simpson's old study?"

"By all means, Smith. A very good idea."

"Yes, sir. It would give us a place where we could work quietly in the evenings."

"Quite so. Quite so."

"Thank you very much, sir. We will move our things in."

"Thank you very much, sir," said Mike.

"Please, sir," shouted Spiller, "aren't I to have it? I'm next on the list, sir. I come next after Simpson. Can't I have it?"

"I'm afraid I have already promised it to Smith, Spiller. You should have spoken before."

"But, sir——"

Psmith eyed the speaker pityingly.

"This tendency to delay, Spiller," he said, "is your besetting fault. Correct it, Edwin. Fight against it."

He turned to Mr. Outwood.

"We should, of course, sir, always be glad to see Spiller in our study. He would always find a cheery welcome waiting there for him. There is no formality between ourselves and Spiller."

"Quite so. An excellent arrangement, Smith. I like

this spirit of comradeship in my house. Then you will be with us on Saturday?"

"On Saturday, sir."

"All this sort of thing, Spiller," said Psmith, as they closed the door, "is very, very trying for a man of culture. Look us up in our study one of these afternoons."

CHAPTER V

GUERRILLA WARFARE

"THERE are few pleasures," said Psmith, as he resumed his favourite position against the mantelpiece and surveyed the commandeered study with the pride of a householder, "keener to the reflective mind than sitting under one's own roof-tree. This place would have been wasted on Spiller; he would not have appreciated it properly."

Mike was finishing his tea. "You're a jolly useful chap to have by you in a crisis, Smith," he said with approval. "We ought to have known each other before."

"The loss was mine," said Psmith courteously. "We will now, with your permission, face the future for a while. I suppose you realize that we are now to a certain extent up against it. Spiller's hot Spanish blood is not going to sit tight and do nothing under a blow like this."

"What can he do? Outwood's given us the study."

"What would you have done if somebody had bagged your study?"

"Made it jolly hot for them!"

"So will Comrade Spiller. I take it that he will collect a gang and make an offensive movement against us directly he can. To all appearances we are in a fairly tight place. It all depends on how big Comrade Spiller's gang will be. I don't like rows, but I'm prepared to take on a reasonable number of assailants in defence of the home."

Mike intimated that he was with him on the point. "The difficulty is, though," he said, "about when we leave this room. I mean, we're all right while we stick here, but we can't stay all night."

"That's just what I was about to point out when you put

it with such admirable clearness. Here we are in a strong-hold, they can only get at us through the door, and we can lock that."

"And jam a chair against it."

"*And*, as you rightly remark, jam a chair against it. But what of the nightfall? What of the time when we retire to our dormitory?"

"Or dormitories. I say, if we're in separate rooms we shall be in the cart."

Psmith eyed Mike with approval. "He thinks of everything! You're the man, Comrade Jackson, to conduct an affair of this kind—such foresight! such resource! We must see to this at once; if they put us in different rooms we're done—we shall be destroyed singly in the watches of the night."

"We'd better nip down to the matron right off."

"Not the matron—Comrade Outwood is the man. We are as sons to him; there is nothing he can deny us. I'm afraid we are quite spoiling his afternoon by these interruptions, but we must rout him out once more."

As they got up, the door handle rattled again, and this time there followed a knocking.

"This must be an emissary of Comrade Spiller's," said Psmith. "Let us parley with the man."

Mike unlocked the door. A light-haired youth with a cheerful, rather vacant face and a receding chin strolled into the room, and stood giggling with his hands in his pockets.

"I just came up to have a look at you," he explained.

"If you move a little to the left," said Psmith, "you will catch the light and shade effects on Jackson's face better."

The newcomer giggled with renewed vigour. "Are you the chap with the eyeglass who jaws all the time?"

"I *do* wear an eyeglass," said Psmith; "as to the rest of the description——"

"My name's Jellicoe."

"Mine is Psmith—P-s-m-i-t-h—one of the Shropshire Psmiths. The object on the skyline is Comrade Jackson."

"Old Spiller," giggled Jellicoe, "is cursing you like

anything downstairs. You *are* chaps! Do you mean to say you simply bagged his study? He's making no end of a row about it."

"Spiller's fiery nature is a byword," said Psmith.

"What's he going to do?" asked Mike, in his practical way.

"He's going to get the chaps to turn you out."

"As I suspected," sighed Psmith, as one mourning over the frailty of human nature. "About how many horny-handed assistants should you say that he would be likely to bring? Will you, for instance, join the glad throng?"

"Me? No fear! I think Spiller's an ass."

"There's nothing like a common thought for binding people together. *I* think Spiller's an ass."

"How many *will* there be, then?" asked Mike.

"He might get about half a dozen, not more, because most of the chaps don't see why they should sweat themselves just because Spiller's study has been bagged."

"Sturdy common sense," said Psmith approvingly, "seems to be the chief virtue of the Sedleigh character."

"We shall be able to tackle a crowd like that," said Mike. "The only thing is we must get into the same dormitory."

"This is where Comrade Jellicoe's knowledge of the local geography will come in useful. Do you happen to know of any snug little room, with, say, about four beds in it? How many dormitories are there?"

"Five—there's one with three beds in it, only it belongs to three chaps."

"I believe in the equal distribution of property. We will go to Comrade Outwood and stake out another claim."

Mr. Outwood received them even more beamingly than before. "Yes, Smith?" he said.

"We must apologise for disturbing you, sir——"

"Not at all, Smith, not at all! I like the boys in my house to come to me when they wish for my advice or help."

"We were wondering, sir, if you would have any objection to Jackson, Jellicoe and myself sharing the dor-

mitory with the three beds in it. A very warm friendship
——" explained Psmith, patting the gurgling Jellicoe
kindly on the shoulder, "has sprung up between Jackson,
Jellicoe and myself."

"You make friends easily, Smith. I like to see it—I like
to see it."

"And we can have the room, sir?"

"Certainly—certainly! Tell the matron as you go
down."

"And now," said Psmith, as they returned to the study,
"we may say that we are in a fairly winning position. A
vote of thanks to Comrade Jellicoe for his valuable assis-
tance."

"You *are* a chap!" said Jellicoe.

The handle began to revolve again.

"That door," said Psmith, "is getting a perfect incubus!
It cuts into one's leisure cruelly."

This time it was a small boy. "They told me to come
up and tell you to come down," he said.

Psmith looked at him searchingly through his eyeglass.

"Who?"

"The senior day-room chaps."

"Spiller?"

"Spiller and Robinson and Stone, and some other
chaps."

"They want us to speak to them?"

"They told me to come up and tell you to come down."

"Go and give Comrade Spiller our compliments and
say that we can't come down, but shall be delighted to
see him up here. Things," he said, as the messenger
departed, "are beginning to move. Better leave the door
open, I think; it will save trouble. Ah, come in, Comrade
Spiller, what can we do for you?"

Spiller advanced into the study; the others waited
outside, crowding in the doorway.

"Look here," said Spiller, "are you going to clear out
of here or not?"

"After Mr. Outwood's kindly thought in giving us the

33

room? You suggest a black and ungrateful action, Comrade Spiller."

"You'll get it hot, if you don't."

"We'll risk it," said Mike.

Jellicoe giggled in the background; the drama in the atmosphere appealed to him. His was a simple and appreciative mind.

"Come on, you chaps," cried Spiller suddenly.

There was an inward rush on the enemy's part, but Mike had been watching. He grabbed Spiller by the shoulders and ran him back against the advancing crowd. For a moment the doorway was blocked, then the weight and impetus of Mike and Spiller prevailed, the enemy gave back, and Mike, stepping into the room again, slammed the door and locked it.

"A neat piece of work," said Psmith approvingly, adjusting his tie at the looking-glass. "The preliminaries may now be considered over, the first shot has been fired. The dogs of war are now loose."

A heavy body crashed against the door.

"They'll have it down," said Jellicoe.

"We must act, Comrade Jackson! Might I trouble you just to turn that key quietly, and the handle, and then to stand by for the next attack."

There was a scrambling of feet in the passage outside, and then a repetition of the onslaught on the door. This time, however, the door, instead of resisting, swung open, and the human battering-ram staggered through into the study. Mike, turning after re-locking the door, was just in time to see Psmith, with a display of energy of which one would not have believed him capable, grip the invader scientifically by an arm and a leg.

Mike jumped to help, but it was needless; the captive was already on the window-sill. As Mike arrived, Psmith dropped him on to the flower-bed below.

Psmith closed the window gently and turned to Jellicoe. "Who was our guest?" he asked, dusting the knees of his trousers where they had pressed against the wall.

34

"Robinson. I say, you *are* a chap!"

"Robinson, was it? Well, we are always glad to see Comrade Robinson, always. I wonder if anybody else is thinking of calling?"

Apparently frontal attack had been abandoned. Whisperings could be heard in the corridor.

Somebody hammered on the door.

"Yes?" called Psmith patiently.

"You'd better come out, you know; you'll only get it hotter if you don't."

"Leave us, Spiller· we would be alone."

A bell rang in the distance.

"Tea," said Jellicoe; "we shall have to go now."

"They won't do anything till after tea, I shouldn't think," said Mike. "There's no harm in going out."

The passage was empty when they opened the door; the call to food was evidently a thing not to be treated lightly by the enemy.

In the dining-room the beleagured garrison were the object of general attention. Everybody turned to look at them as they came in. It was plain that the study episode had been a topic of conversation. Spiller's face was crimson, and Robinson's coat sleeve still bore traces of garden mould.

Mike felt rather conscious of the eyes, but Psmith was in his element. His demeanour throughout the meal was that of some whimsical monarch condescending for a freak to revel with his humble subjects.

Towards the end of the meal Psmith scribbled a note and passed it to Mike. It read: "Directly this is over, nip upstairs as quickly as you can."

Mike followed the advice; they were first out of the room. When they had been in the study a few moments, Jellicoe knocked at the door. "Lucky you two cut away so quick," he said. "They were going to try and get you into the senior day-room and scrag you there."

"This," said Psmith, leaning against the mantelpiece, "is exciting, but it can't go on. We have got for our

35

sins to be in this place for a whole term, and if we are going to do the Hunted Fawn business all the time, life in the true sense of the word will become an impossibility. My nerves are so delicately attuned that the strain would simply reduce them to hash. We are not prepared to carry on a long campaign—the thing must be settled at once."

"Shall we go down to the senior day-room, and have it out?" said Mike.

"No, we will play the fixture on our own ground. I think we may take it as tolerably certain that Comrade Spiller and his hired ruffians will try to corner us in the dormitory tonight. Well, of course, we could fake up some sort of barricade for the door, but then we should have all the trouble over again tomorrow and the day after that. Personally I don't propose to be chivvied about indefinitely like this, so I propose that we let them come into the dormitory, and see what happens. Is this meeting with me?"

"I think that's sound," said Mike. "We needn't drag Jellicoe into it."

"As a matter of fact—if you don't mind——" began that man of peace.

"Quite right," said Psmith; "this is not Comrade Jellicoe's scene at all; he has got to spend the term in the senior day-room, whereas we have our little wooden *châlet* to retire to in times of stress. Comrade Jellicoe must stand out of the game altogether. We shall be glad of his moral support, but otherwise, *ne pas*. And now, as there won't be anything doing till bedtime, I think I'll collar this table and write home and tell my people that all is well with their Rupert."

CHAPTER VI

UNPLEASANTNESS IN THE SMALL HOURS

JELLICOE, that human encyclopædia, consulted on the probable movements of the enemy, deposed that Spiller, retiring at ten, would make for Dormitory One in the same passage, where Robinson also had a bed. The rest of the opposing forces were distributed among other and more distant rooms. It was probable, therefore, that Dormitory One would be the rendezvous. As to the time when an attack might be expected, it was unlikely that it would occur before half-past eleven. Mr. Outwood went the round of the dormitories at eleven.

"And touching," said Psmith, "the matter of noise, must this business be conducted in a subdued and *sotto voce* manner, or may we let ourselves go a bit here and there?"

"I shouldn't think old Outwood's likely to hear you —he sleeps miles away on the other side of the house. He never hears anything. We often rag half the night and nothing happens."

"This appears to be a thoroughly nice, well-conducted establishment. What would my mother say if she could see her Rupert in the midst of these reckless youths!"

"All the better," said Mike; "we don't want anybody butting in and stopping the show before it's half started."

"Comrade Jackson's Berserk blood is up—I can hear it sizzling. I quite agree these things are all very disturbing and painful, but it's as well to do them thoroughly when one's once in for them. Is there nobody else who might interfere with our gambols?"

"Barnes might," said Jellicoe, "only he won't."

"Who is Barnes?"

"Head of the house—a rotter. He's in a funk of Stone and Robinson; they rag him; he'll simply sit tight."

"Then I think," said Psmith placidly, "we may look forward to a very pleasant evening. Shall we be moving?"

Mr. Outwood paid his visit at eleven, as predicted by Jellicoe, beaming vaguely into the darkness over a torch, and disappeared again, closing the door.

"How about that door?" said Mike. "Shall we leave it open for them?"

"Not so, but far otherwise. If it's shut we shall hear them at it when they come. Subject to your approval, Comrade Jackson, I have evolved the following plan of action. I always ask myself on these occasions, 'What would Napoleon have done?' I think Napoleon would have sat in a chair by his wash-hand stand, which is close to the door; he would have posted you by your wash-hand stand, and he would have instructed Comrade Jellicoe, directly he heard the door-handle turned, to give his celebrated imitation of a dormitory breathing heavily in its sleep. He would then——"

"I tell you what," said Mike, "how about tying a string at the top of the steps?"

"Yes, Napoleon would have done that, too. Hats off to Comrade Jackson, the man with the big brain!"

The floor of the dormitory was below the level of the door. There were three steps leading down to it. Psmith switched on his torch and they examined the ground. The leg of a wardrobe and the leg of Jellicoe's bed made it possible for the string to be fastened in a satisfactory manner across the lower step. Psmith surveyed the result with approval.

"Dashed neat!" he said. "Practically the sunken road which dished the Cuirassiers at Waterloo. I seem to see Comrade Spiller coming one of the finest purlers in the world's history."

"If they've got a torch——"

"They won't have. If they have, stand by and grab it at once; then they'll charge forward and all will be well.

If they have no light, fire into the brown with a jug of water. Lest we forget, I'll collar Comrade Jellicoe's jug now and keep it handy. A couple of sheets would also not be amiss—we will enmesh the enemy!"

"Right ho!" said Mike.

"These humane preparations being concluded," said Psmith, "we will retire to our posts and wait. Comrade Jellicoe, don't forget to breathe like an asthmatic sheep when you hear the door opened; they may wait at the top of the steps, listening."

"You *are* a lad!" said Jellicoe.

Waiting in the dark for something to happen is always a trying experience, especially if, as on this occasion, silence is essential. Mike was tired after his journey, and he had begun to doze when he was jerked back to wakefulness by the stealthy turning of the door-handle; the faintest rustle from Psmith's direction followed, and a slight giggle, succeeded by a series of deep breaths, showed that Jellicoe, too, had heard the noise.

There was a creaking sound.

It was pitch-dark in the dormitory, but Mike could follow the invaders' movements as clearly as if it had been broad daylight. They had opened the door and were listening. Jellicoe's breathing grew more asthmatic; he was flinging himself into his part with the whole-heartedness of the true artist.

The creak was followed by a sound of whispering, then another creak. The enemy had advanced to the top step. . . . Another creak. . . . The vanguard had reached the second step. . . . In another moment——

CRASH!

And at that point the proceedings may be said to have formally opened.

A struggling mass bumped against Mike's shins as he rose from his chair; he emptied his jug on to this mass, and a yell of anguish showed that the contents had got to the right address.

Then a hand grabbed his ankle and he went down, a

million sparks dancing before his eyes as a fist, flying out at a venture, caught him on the nose.

Mike had not been well-disposed towards the invaders before, but now he ran amok, hitting out right and left at random. His right missed, but his left went home hard on some portion of somebody's anatomy. A kick freed his ankle and he staggered to his feet. At the same moment a sudden increase in the general volume of noise spoke eloquently of good work that was being put in by Psmith.

Even at that crisis, Mike could not help feeling that if a row of this calibre did not draw Mr. Outwood from his bed, he must be an unusual kind of house-master.

He plunged forward again with outstretched arms, and stumbled and fell over one of the on-the-floor section of the opposing force. They seized each other earnestly and rolled across the room till Mike, contriving to secure his adversary's head, bumped it on the floor with such abandon that, with a muffled yell, the other let go, and for the second time he rose. As he did so he was conscious of a curious thudding sound that made itself heard through the other assorted noises of the battle.

All this time the fight had gone on in the blackest darkness, but now a light shone on the proceedings. Interested occupants of other dormitories, roused from their slumbers, had come to observe the sport. They had switched on the light and were crowding in the doorway.

By the light of this Mike got a swift view of the theatre of war. The enemy appeared to number five. The warrior whose head Mike had bumped on the floor was Robinson, who was sitting up feeling his skull in a gingerly fashion. To Mike's right, almost touching him, was Stone. In the direction of the door, Psmith, wielding in his right hand the cord of a dressing-gown, was engaging the remaining three with a patient smile. They were clad in pyjamas, and appeared to be feeling the dressing-gown cord acutely.

The sudden light dazed both sides momentarily. The defence was the first to recover, Mike, with a swing, upsetting Stone, and Psmith, having seized and emptied

Jellicoe's jug over Spiller, getting to work again with the cord in a manner that roused the utmost enthusiasm of the spectators.

Agility seemed to be the leading feature of Psmith's tactics. He was everywhere—on Mike's bed, on his own, on Jellicoe's (drawing a passionate complaint from that non-combatant, on whose face he inadvertently trod), on the floor—he ranged the room, sowing destruction.

The enemy were disheartened; they had started with the idea that this was to be a surprise attack, and it was disconcerting to find the garrison armed at all points. Gradually they edged to the door, and a final rush sent them through.

"Hold the door for a second," cried Psmith, and vanished. Mike was alone in the doorway.

It was a situation which exactly suited his frame of mind; he stood alone in direct opposition to the community into which Fate had pitchforked him so abruptly. He liked the feeling; for the first time since his father had given him his views upon school reports that morning in the Easter holidays, he felt satisfied with life. He hoped, outnumbered as he was, that the enemy would come on again and not give the thing up in disgust; he wanted more.

On an occasion like this there is rarely anything approaching concerted action on the part of the aggressors. When the attack came, it was not a combined attack; Stone, who was nearest to the door, made a sudden dash forward, and Mike hit him under the chin.

Stone drew back, and there was another interval for rest and reflection.

It was interrupted by the reappearance of Psmith, who strolled back along the passage swinging his dressing-gown cord as if it were some clouded cane.

"Sorry to keep you waiting, Comrade Jackson," he said politely. "Duty called me elsewhere. With the kindly aid of a guide who knows the lie of the land, I have been making a short tour of the dormitories. I have poured divers jugfuls of water over Comrade Spiller's bed, Comrade

Robinson's bed, Comrade Stone's—Spiller, Spiller, these are harsh words; where you pick them up I can't think—not from me. Well, well, I suppose there must be an end to the pleasantest of functions. Good night, good night."

The door closed behind Mike and himself. For ten minutes shufflings and whisperings went on in the corridor, but nobody touched the handle.

Then there was a sound of retreating footsteps, and silence reigned.

On the following morning there was a notice on the house-board. It ran:

INDOOR GAMES

Dormitory-raiders are informed that in future neither Mr. Psmith nor Mr. Jackson will be at home to visitors. This nuisance must now cease.

R. PSMITH.
M. JACKSON.

CHAPTER VII

ADAIR

O^N the same morning Mike met Adair for the first time.

He was going across to school with Psmith and Jellicoe, when a group of three came out of the gate of the house next door.

"That's Adair," said Jellicoe, "in the middle."

His voice had assumed a tone almost of awe.

"Who's Adair?" asked Mike.

"Captain of cricket, and lots of other things."

Mike could only see the celebrity's back. He had broad shoulders and wiry, light hair, almost white. He walked well, as if he were used to running. Altogether a fit-looking sort of man. Even Mike's jaundiced eye saw that.

As a matter of fact, Adair deserved more than a casual glance. He was that rare type, the natural leader. Many boys and men, if accident, or the passage of time, places them in a position where they are expected to lead, can handle the job without disaster; but that is a very different thing from being a born leader. Adair was of the sort that comes to the top by sheer force of character and determination. He was not naturally clever at work, but he had gone at it with a dogged resolution which had carried him up the school, and landed him high in the Sixth. As a cricketer he was almost entirely self-taught. Nature had given him a good eye, and left the thing at that. Adair's doggedness had triumphed over her failure to do her work thoroughly. At the cost of more trouble than most people give to their life-work he had made himself into a bowler. He read the authorities, and watched first-class players, and thought the thing out on his own account, and he divided the art of bowling into three sections. First, and most important—pitch. Second on the list—break. Third —pace. He set himself to acquire pitch. He acquired it. Bowling at his own pace and without any attempt at break, he could now drop the ball on an envelope seven times out of ten.

Break was a more uncertain quantity. Sometimes he could get it at the expense of pitch, sometimes at the expense of pace. Some days he could get all three, and then he was an uncommonly bad man to face on anything but a plumb wicket.

Running he had acquired in a similar manner. He had nothing approaching style, but he had twice won the mile and half-mile at the Sports off elegant runners, who knew all about stride and the correct timing of the sprints and all the rest of it.

Briefly, he was a worker. He had heart.

A boy of Adair's type is always a force in a school. In a big public school of six or seven hundred, his influence is felt less; but in a small school like Sedleigh he is like a tidal wave, sweeping all before him. There were two hundred boys at Sedleigh, and there was not one of them in all probability who had not, directly or indirectly, been influenced by Adair. As a small boy his sphere was not large, but the effects of his work began to be apparent even then. It is human nature to want to get something which somebody else obviously values very much; and when it was observed by members of his form that Adair was going to great trouble and inconvenience to secure a place in the form eleven or fifteen, they naturally began to think, too, that it was worth being in those teams. The consequence was that his form always played hard. This made other forms play hard. And the net result was that, when Adair succeeded to the captaincy of Rugger and cricket in the same year, Sedleigh, as Mr. Downing, Adair's house-master and the nearest approach to a cricket-master that Sedleigh

44

possessed, had a fondness for saying, was a keen school. As a whole, it both worked and played with energy.

All it wanted now was opportunity.

This Adair was determined to give it. He had that passionate fondness for his school which every boy is popularly supposed to have, but which really is implanted in about one in every thousand. The average public-school boy *likes* his school. He hopes it will lick Bedford at Rugger and Malvern at cricket, but he rather bets it won't. He is sorry to leave, and he likes going back at the end of the holidays, but as for any passionate, deep-seated love of the place, he would think it rather bad form than otherwise. If anybody came up to him, slapped him on the back, and cried, "Come along, Jenkins, my boy! Play up for the old school, Jenkins! The dear old school! The old place you love so!" he would feel seriously ill.

Adair was the exception.

To Adair, Sedleigh was almost a religion. Both his parents were dead; his guardian, with whom he spent the holidays, was a man with neuralgia at one end of him and gout at the other; and the only really pleasant times Adair had had, as far back as he could remember, he owed to Sedleigh. The place had grown on him, absorbed him. Where Mike, violently transplanted from Wrykyn, saw only a wretched little hole not to be mentioned in the same breath with Wrykyn, Adair, dreaming of the future, saw a colossal establishment, a public school among public schools, a lump of human radium, shooting out Blues and Balliol Scholars year after year without ceasing.

It would not be so till long after he was gone and forgotten, but he did not mind that. His devotion to Sedleigh was purely unselfish. He did not want fame. All he worked for was that the school should grow and grow, keener and better at games and more prosperous year by year, till it should take its rank among *the* schools, and to be an Old Sedleighan should be a badge passing its owner everywhere.

"He's captain of cricket and Rugger," said Jellicoe

45

impressively. "He's in the shooting eight. He's won the mile and half-mile two years running. He would have boxed at Aldershot last term, only he sprained his wrist. And he plays fives jolly well!"

"Sort of little tin god," said Mike, taking a violent dislike to Adair from that moment.

Mike's actual acquaintance with this all-round man dated from the dinner-hour that day. Mike was walking to the house with Psmith. Psmith was a little ruffled on account of a slight passage-of-arms he had had with his form-master during morning school.

"'There's a P before the Smith,' I said to him. 'Ah, P. Smith, I see,' replied the goat. 'Not Peasmith,' I replied, exercising wonderful self-restraint, 'just Psmith.' It took me ten minutes to drive the thing into the man's head; and when I *had* driven it in, he sent me out of the room for looking at him through my eyeglass. Comrade Jackson, I fear me we have fallen among bad men. I suspect that we are going to be much persecuted by scoundrels."

"Both you chaps play cricket, I suppose?"

They turned. It was Adair. Seeing him face to face, Mike was aware of a pair of very bright blue eyes and a square jaw. In any other place and mood he would have liked Adair at sight. His prejudice, however, against all things Sedleighan was too much for him. "I don't," he said shortly.

"Haven't you *ever* played?"

"My little sister and I sometimes play with a soft ball at home."

Adair looked sharply at him. A temper was evidently one of his numerous qualities.

"Oh," he said. "Well, perhaps you wouldn't mind turning out this afternoon and seeing what you can do with a hard ball—if you can manage without your little sister."

"I should think the form at this place would be about on a level with hers. But I don't happen to be playing cricket, as I think I told you."

46

Adair's jaw grew squarer than ever. Mike was wearing a gloomy scowl.

Psmith joined suavely in the dialogue.

"My dear old comrades," he said, "don't let us brawl over this matter. This is a time for the honeyed word, the kindly eye, and the pleasant smile. Let me explain to Comrade Adair. Speaking for Comrade Jackson and myself, we should both be delighted to join in the mimic warfare of our National Game, as you suggest, only the fact is, we happen to be the Young Archæologists. We gave in our names last night. When you are being carried back to the pavilion after your century against Loamshire—do you play Loamshire?—we shall be grubbing in the hard ground for ruined abbeys. The old choice between Pleasure and Duty, Comrade Adair. A Boy's Cross-Roads."

"Then you won't play?"

"No," said Mike.

"Archæology," said Psmith, with a deprecatory wave of the hand, "will brook no divided allegiance from her devotees."

Adair turned, and walked on.

Scarcely had he gone, when another voice hailed them with precisely the same question.

"Both you fellows are going to play cricket, eh?"

It was a master. A short, wiry little man with a sharp nose and a general resemblance, both in manner and appearance, to an excitable bullfinch.

"I saw Adair speaking to you. I suppose you will both play. I like every new boy to begin at once. The more new blood we have, the better. We want keenness here. We are, above all, a keen school. I want every boy to be keen."

"We are, sir," said Psmith, with fervour.

"Excellent."

"On archæology."

Mr. Downing—for it was no less a celebrity—started, as one who perceives a loathly caterpillar in his salad.

"Archæology!"

47

"We gave in our names to Mr. Outwood last night, sir. Archæology is a passion with us, sir. When we heard that there was a society here, we went singing about the house."

"I call it an unnatural pursuit for boys," said Mr. Downing vehemently. "I don't like it. I tell you I don't like it. It is not for me to interfere with one of my colleagues on the staff, but I tell you frankly that in my opinion it is an abominable waste of time for a boy. It gets him into idle, loafing habits."

"I never loaf, sir," said Psmith.

"I was not alluding to you in particular. I was referring to the principle of the thing. A boy ought to be playing cricket with other boys, not wandering at large about the country, probably smoking and going into low public-houses."

"A very wild lot, sir, I fear, the Archæological Society here," sighed Psmith, shaking his head.

"If you choose to waste your time, I suppose I can't hinder you. But in my opinion it is foolery, nothing else."

He stumped off.

"Now *he's* cross," said Psmith, looking after him. "I'm afraid we're getting ourselves disliked here."

"Good job, too."

"At any rate, Comrade Outwood loves us. Let's go on and see what sort of a lunch that large-hearted fossil-fancier is going to give us."

CHAPTER VIII

MIKE FINDS OCCUPATION

THERE was more than one moment during the first fortnight of term when Mike found himself regretting the attitude he had imposed upon himself with regard to Sedleighan cricket. He began to realize the eternal truth of the proverb about half a loaf and no bread. In the first flush of his resentment against his new surroundings he had refused to play cricket. And now he positively ached for a game. Any sort of a game. An innings for a Kindergarten *v.* the Second Eleven of a Home of Rest for Centenarians would have soothed him. There were times, when the sun shone, and he caught sight of white flannels on a green ground, and heard the "plonk" of bat striking ball, when he felt like rushing to Adair and shouting, "I *will* be good. I was in the Wrykyn team three years, and had an average of over fifty the last two seasons. Lead me to the nearest net, and let me feel a bat in my hands again."

But every time he shrank from such a climb down. It couldn't be done.

What made it worse was that he saw, after watching behind the nets once or twice, that Sedleigh cricket was not the childish burlesque of the game which he had been rash enough to assume that it must be. Numbers do not make good cricket. They only make the presence of good cricketers more likely, by the law of averages.

Mike soon saw that cricket was by no means an unknown art at Sedleigh. Adair, to begin with, was a very good bowler indeed. He was not a Burgess, but Burgess was the only Wrykyn bowler whom, in his three years' experience of the school, Mike would have placed above him. He was a long way better than Neville-Smith, and Wyatt, and Milton, and the others who had taken wickets for Wrykyn.

The batting was not so good, but there were some quite capable men. Barnes, the head of Outwood's, he who preferred not to interfere with Stone and Robinson, was a mild, rather timid-looking youth—not unlike what Mr. Outwood must have been as a boy—but he knew how to keep balls out of his wicket. He was a good bat of the old plodding type.

Stone and Robinson themselves, that swashbuckling pair, who now treated Mike and Psmith with cold but consistent politeness, were both fair batsmen, and Stone was a good slow bowler.

There were other exponents of the game, mostly in Downing's house.

Altogether, quite worthy colleagues even for a man who had been a star at Wrykyn.

One solitary overture Mike made during that first fortnight. He did not repeat the experiment.

It was on a Thursday afternoon, after school. The day was warm, but freshened by an almost imperceptible breeze. The air was full of the scent of the cut grass which lay in little heaps behind the nets. This is the real cricket scent, which calls to one like the very voice of the game.

Mike, as he sat there watching, could stand it no longer.

He went up to Adair.

"May I have an innings at this net?" he asked. He was embarrassed and nervous, and was trying not to show it. The natural result was that his manner was offensively abrupt.

Adair was taking off his pads after his innings. He looked up. "This net," it may be observed, was the first eleven net.

"What?" he said.

Mike repeated his request. More abruptly this time, from increased embarrassment.

"This is the first eleven net," said Adair coldly. "Go in after Lodge over there."

"Over there" was the end net, where frenzied novices were bowling on a corrugated pitch to a red-haired youth with enormous feet, who looked as if he were taking his first lesson at the game.

Mike walked away without a word.

The Archæological Society expeditions, even though they carried with them the privilege of listening to Psmith's views of life, proved but a poor substitute for cricket. Psmith, who had no counter-attraction shouting to him that he ought to be elsewhere, seemed to enjoy them hugely, but Mike almost cried sometimes from boredom. It was not always possible to slip away from the throng, for Mr. Outwood evidently looked upon them as among the very faithful, and kept them by his side.

Mike on these occasions was silent and jumpy, his brow "sicklied o'er with the pale cast of care." But Psmith followed his leader with the pleased and indulgent air of a father whose infant son is showing him round the garden. Psmith's attitude towards archæological research struck a new note in the history of that neglected science. He was amiable, but patronizing. He patronized fossils, and he patronized ruins. If he had been confronted with the Great Pyramid, he would have patronized that.

He seemed to be consumed by a thirst for knowledge.

That this was not altogether a genuine thirst was proved in the third expedition. Mr. Outwood and his band were pecking away at the site of an old Roman camp. Psmith approached Mike.

"Having inspired confidence," he said, "by the docility of our demeanour, let us slip away, and brood apart for awhile. Roman camps, to be absolutely accurate, give me the pip. And I never want to see another putrid fossil in my life. Let us find some shady nook where a man may lie on his back for a bit."

Mike, over whom the proceedings connected with the

Roman camp had long since begun to shed a blue depression, offered no opposition, and they strolled away down the hill.

Looking back, they saw that the archæologists were still hard at it. Their departure had passed unnoticed.

"A fatiguing pursuit, this grubbing for mementoes of the past," said Psmith. "And, above all, dashed bad for the knees of the trousers. Mine are like some furrowed field. It's a great grief to a man of refinement, I can tell you, Comrade Jackson. Ah, this looks a likely spot."

They had passed through a gate into the field beyond. At the farther end there was a brook, shaded by trees and running with a pleasant sound over pebbles.

"Thus far," said Psmith, hitching up the knees of his trousers, and sitting down, "and no farther. We will rest here awhile, and listen to the music of the brook. In fact, unless you have anything important to say, I rather think I'll go to sleep. In this busy life of ours these naps by the wayside are invaluable. Call me in about an hour." And Psmith, heaving the comfortable sigh of the worker who by toil has earned rest, lay down, with his head against a mossy tree-stump, and closed his eyes.

Mike sat on for a few minutes, listening to the water and making centuries in his mind, and then, finding this a little dull, he got up, jumped the brook, and began to explore the wood on the other side.

He had not gone many yards when a dog emerged suddenly from the undergrowth, and began to bark vigorously at him.

Mike liked dogs, and, on acquaintance, they always liked him. But when you meet a dog in someone else's wood, it is as well not to stop in order that you may get to understand each other. Mike began to thread his way back through the trees.

He was too late.

"Stop! What the dickens are you doing here?" shouted a voice behind him.

In the same situation a few years before, Mike would

have carried on, and trusted to speed to save him. But now there seemed a lack of dignity in the action. He came back to where the man was standing.

"I'm sorry if I'm trespassing," he said. "I was just having a look round."

"The dickens you— Why, you're Jackson!"

Mike looked at him. He was a short, broad young man with a fair moustache. Mike knew that he had seen him before somewhere, but he could not place him.

"I played against you, for the Free Foresters last summer. In passing, you seem to be a bit of a free forester yourself, dancing in among my nesting pheasants."

"I'm frightfully sorry."

"That's all right. Where do you spring from?"

"Of course—I remember you now. You're Prendergast. You made fifty-eight not out."

"Thanks. I was afraid the only thing you would remember about me was that you took a century mostly off my bowling."

"You ought to have had me second ball, only cover dropped it."

"Don't rake up forgotten tragedies. How is it you're not at Wrykyn? What are you doing down here?"

"I've left Wrykyn."

Prendergast suddenly changed the conversation. When a fellow tells you that he has left school unexpectedly, it is not always tactful to inquire the reason. He began to talk about himself.

"I hang out down here. I do a little farming and a good deal of pottering about."

"Get any cricket?" asked Mike, turning to the subject next his heart.

"Only village. Very keen, but no great shakes. By the way, how are you off for cricket now? Have you ever got a spare afternoon?"

Mike's heart leaped.

"Any Wednesday or Saturday. Look here, I'll tell you how it is."

And he told how matters stood with him.

"So, you see," he concluded, "I'm supposed to be hunting for ruins and things"—Mike's ideas on the subject of archæology were vague—"but I could always slip away. We all start out together, but I could nip back, get on to my bike—I've got it down here—and meet you anywhere you liked. By Jove, I'm simply dying for a game. I can hardly keep my hands off a bat."

"I'll give you all you want. What you'd better do is to ride straight to Lower Borlock—that's the name of the place—and I'll meet you on the ground. Anyone will tell you where Lower Borlock is. It's just off the London road. There's a signpost where you turn off. Can you come next Saturday?"

"Rather. I suppose you can fix me up with a bat and pads? I don't want to bring mine."

"I'll lend you everything. I say, you know, we can't give you a Wrykyn wicket. The Lower Borlock pitch isn't a shirt-front."

"I'll play on a rockery, if you want me to," said Mike.

"You're going to what?" asked Psmith, sleepily, on being awakened and told the news.

"I'm going to play cricket, for a village near here. I say, don't tell a soul, will you? I don't want it to get about, or I may get lugged in to play for the school."

"My lips are sealed. I think I'll come and watch you. Cricket I dislike, but watching cricket is one of the finest of Britain's manly sports. I'll borrow Jellicoe's bicycle."

That Saturday, Lower Borlock smote the men of Chidford hip and thigh. Their victory was due to a hurricane innings of seventy-five by a newcomer to the team, M. Jackson.

CHAPTER IX

THE FIRE BRIGADE MEETING

CRICKET is the great safety-valve. If you like the game, and are in a position to play it at least twice a week, life can never be entirely grey. As time went on, and his average for Lower Borlock reached the fifties and stayed there, Mike began, though he would not have admitted it, to enjoy himself. It was not Wrykyn, but it was a very decent substitute.

The only really considerable element making for discomfort now was Mr. Downing. By bad luck it was in his form that Mike had been placed on arrival; and Mr. Downing, never an easy form-master to get on with, proved more than usually difficult in his dealings with Mike.

They had taken a dislike to each other at their first meeting; and it grew with further acquaintance. To Mike, Mr. Downing was all that a master ought not to be, fussy, pompous, and openly influenced in his official dealings with his form by his own private likes and dislikes. To Mr. Downing, Mike was simply an unamiable loafer, who did nothing for the school and apparently had none of the healthy instincts which should be implanted in the healthy boy. Mr. Downing was rather strong on the healthy boy.

The two lived in a state of simmering hostility, punctuated at intervals by crises, which usually resulted in Lower Borlock having to play some unskilled labourer in place of their star batsman, employed doing "overtime."

One of the most acute of these crises, and the most important, in that it was the direct cause of Mike's appearance in Sedleigh cricket, had to do with the third weekly meeting of the School Fire Brigade.

It may be remembered that this well-supported institution was under Mr. Downing's special care. It was, indeed, his pet hobby and the apple of his eye.

Just as you had to join the Archæological Society to secure the esteem of Mr. Outwood, so to become a member of the Fire Brigade was a safe passport to the regard of Mr. Downing. To show a keenness for cricket was good, but to join the Fire Brigade was best of all.

The Brigade was carefully organized. At its head was Mr. Downing, a sort of high priest; under him was a captain, and under the captain a vice-captain. These two officials were those sportive allies, Stone and Robinson, of Outwood's house, who, having perceived at a very early date the gorgeous opportunities for ragging which the Brigade offered to its members, had joined young and worked their way up.

Under them were the rank and file, about thirty in all, of whom perhaps seven were earnest workers, who looked on the Brigade in the right, or Downing, spirit. The rest were entirely frivolous.

The weekly meetings were always full of life and excitement.

At this point it is as well to introduce Sammy to the reader.

Sammy, short for Sampson, was a young bull-terrier belonging to Mr. Downing. If it is possible for a man to have two apples of his eye, Sammy was the other. He was a large, light-hearted dog with a white coat, an engaging expression, the tongue of an ant-eater, and a manner which was a happy blend of hurricane and circular saw. He had long legs, a tenor voice, and was apparently made of india-rubber.

Sammy was a great favourite in the school, and a particular friend of Mike's, the Wrykynian being always a firm ally of every dog he met after two minutes' acquaintance.

In passing, Jellicoe owned a clockwork rat, much in request during French lessons.

We will now proceed to the painful details.

The meetings of the Fire Brigade were held after school in Mr. Downing's form-room. The proceedings always began in the same way, by the reading of the minutes of the last meeting. After that the entertainment varied according to whether the members happened to be fertile or not in ideas for the disturbing of the peace.

Today they were in very fair form.

As soon as Mr. Downing had closed the minute-book, Wilson, of the School House, held up his hand.

"Well, Wilson?"

"Please, sir, couldn't we have a uniform for the Brigade?"

"A uniform?" Mr. Downing pondered.

"Red, with green stripes, sir."

Red, with a thin green stripe, was the Sedleigh colour.

"Shall I put it to the vote, sir?" asked Stone.

"One moment, Stone."

"Those in favour of the motion move to the left, those against it to the right."

A scuffling of feet, a slamming of desk-lids and an upset blackboard, and the meeting had divided.

Mr. Downing rapped irritably on his desk.

"Sit down!" he said. "Sit down! I won't have this noise and disturbance. Stone, sit down—Wilson, get back to your place."

"Please, sir, the motion is carried by twenty-five votes to six."

"Please, sir, may I go and get measured this evening?"

"Please, sir——"

"Si-*lence*! The idea of a uniform is, of course, out of the question."

"Oo-oo-oo-oo, sir-r-r!"

"Be *quiet*! Entirely out of the question. We cannot plunge into needless expense. Stone, listen to me. I cannot have this noise and disturbance! Another time when a point arises it must be settled by a show of hands. Well, Wilson?"

"Please, sir, may we have helmets?"

"Very useful as a protection against falling timbers, sir," said Robinson.

"I don't think my people would be pleased, sir, if they knew I was going out to fires without a helmet," said Stone.

The whole strength of the company: "Please, sir, may we have helmets?"

"Those in favour——" began Stone.

Mr. Downing banged on his desk. "Silence! Silence!! Silence!!! Helmets are, of course, perfectly preposterous."

"Oo-oo-oo-oo, sir-r-r!"

"But, sir, the danger!"

"Please, sir, the falling timbers!"

The Fire Brigade had been in action once and once only in the memory of man, and that time it was a haystack which had burnt itself out just as the rescuers had succeeded in fastening the hose to the hydrant.

"Silence!"

"Then, please, sir, couldn't we have an honour cap? It wouldn't be expensive, and it would be just as good as a helmet for all the timbers that are likely to fall on our heads."

Mr. Downing smiled a wry smile.

"Our Wilson is facetious," he remarked frostily.

"Sir, no, sir! I wasn't facetious! Or couldn't we have tasselled caps like the first fifteen have? They——"

"Wilson, leave the room!"

"Sir, *please*, sir!"

"This moment, Wilson. And," as he reached the door, "do me one hundred lines."

A pained "OO-oo-oo, sir-r-r," was cut off by the closing door.

Mr. Downing proceeded to improve the occasion. "I deplore this growing spirit of flippancy," he said. "I tell you I deplore it! It is not right! If this Fire Brigade is to be of solid use, there must be less of this flippancy. We

must have keenness.   I want you boys above all to be keen.
I—— What is that noise?"

From the other side of the door proceeded a sound
like water gurgling from a bottle, mingled with cries half-
suppressed, as if somebody were being prevented from
uttering them by a hand laid over his mouth.   The sufferer
appeared to have a high voice.

There was a tap at the door and Mike walked in.   He
was not alone.   Those near enough to see, saw that he was
accompanied by Jellicoe's clockwork rat, which moved
rapidly over the floor in the direction of the opposite
wall.

"May I fetch a book from my desk, sir?" asked Mike.

"Very well—be quick, Jackson; we are busy."

Being interrupted in one of his addresses to the Brigade
irritated Mr. Downing.

The muffled cries grew more distinct.

"What—is—that—noise?" shrilled Mr. Downing.

"Noise, sir?" asked Mike, puzzled.

"I think it's something outside the window, sir," said
Stone helpfully.

"A bird, I think, sir," said Robinson.

"Don't be absurd!" snapped Mr. Downing.   "It's
outside the door.   Wilson!"

"Yes, sir?" said a voice "off."

"Are you making that whining noise?"

"Whining noise, sir?   No, sir, I'm not making a
whining noise."

"What *sort* of noise, sir?" inquired Mike, as many
Wrykynians had asked before him.   It was a question
invented by Wrykyn for use in just such a case as this.

"I do not propose," said Mr. Downing acidly "to imitate
the noise; you can all hear it perfectly plainly.   It is a
curious whining noise."

"They are mowing the cricket field, sir," said the
invisible Wilson.   "Perhaps that's it."

"It may be one of the desks squeaking, sir," put in
Stone.   "They do sometimes."

"Or somebody's shoes, sir," added Robinson.

"Silence! Wilson?"

"Yes, sir?" bellowed the unseen one.

"Don't shout at me from the corridor like that. Come in."

"Yes, sir!"

As he spoke the muffled whining changed suddenly to a series of tenor shrieks, and the india-rubber form of Sammy bounded into the room like an excited kangaroo.

Willing hands had by this time deflected the clockwork rat from the wall to which it had been steering, and pointed it up the alley-way between the two rows of desks. Mr. Downing, rising from his place, was just in time to see Sammy with a last leap spring on his prey and begin worrying it.

Chaos reigned.

"A rat!" shouted Robinson.

The twenty-three members of the Brigade who were not earnest instantly dealt with the situation, each in the manner that seemed proper to him. Some leaped on to forms, others flung books, all shouted. It was a stirring, bustling scene.

Sammy had by this time disposed of the clockwork rat, and was now standing, like Marius, among the ruins barking triumphantly.

The banging on Mr. Downing's desk resembled thunder. It rose above all the other noises till in time they gave up the competition and died away.

Mr. Downing shot out orders, threats, and penalties with the rapidity of a Bren gun.

"Stone, sit down! Donovan, if you do not sit down, you will be severely punished. Henderson, one hundred lines for gross disorder! Windham, the same! Go to your seat, Vincent. What are you doing, Broughton-Knight? I will not have this disgraceful noise and disorder! The meeting is at an end; go quietly from the room, all of you. Jackson and Wilson, remain. *Quietly*, I said, Durand! Don't shuffle your feet in that abominable way."

Crash!

"Wolferstan, I distinctly saw you upset that blackboard with a movement of your hand—one hundred lines. Go quietly from the room, everybody."

The meeting dispersed.

"Jackson and Wilson, come here. What's the meaning of this disgraceful conduct? Put that dog out of the room, Jackson."

Mike removed the yelling Sammy and shut the door on him.

"Well, Wilson?"

"Please, sir, I was playing with a clockwork rat——"

"What business have you to be playing with clockwork rats?"

"Then I remembered," said Mike, "that I had left my Horace in my desk, so I came in——"

"And by a fluke, sir," said Wilson, as one who tells of strange things, "the rat happened to be pointing in the same direction, so he came in, too."

"I met Sammy on the gravel outside and he followed me."

"I tried to collar him, but when you told me to come in, sir, I had to let him go, and he came in after the rat."

It was plain to Mr. Downing that the burden of sin was shared equally by both culprits. Wilson had supplied the rat, Mike the dog; but Mr. Downing liked Wilson and disliked Mike. Wilson was in the Fire Brigade, frivolous at times, it was true, but nevertheless a member. Also he kept wicket for the school. Mike was a member of the Archæological Society, and had refused to play cricket.

Mr. Downing allowed these facts to influence him in passing sentence.

"One hundred lines, Wilson," he said. "You may go."

Wilson departed with the air of a man who has had a great deal of fun, and paid very little for it.

Mr. Downing turned to Mike. "You will stay in on Saturday afternoon, Jackson; it will interfere with your

Archæological studies, I fear, but it may teach you that we have no room at Sedleigh for boys who spend their time loafing about and making themselves a nuisance. We are a keen school; this is no place for boys who do nothing but waste their time. That will do, Jackson."

And Mr. Downing walked out of the room. In affairs of this kind a master has a habit of getting the last word.

CHAPTER X

ACHILLES LEAVES HIS TENT

THEY say misfortunes never come singly. As Mike
sat brooding over his wrongs in his study, after the
Sammy incident, Jellicoe came into the room, and, without
preamble, asked for the loan of a pound.

When one has been in the habit of confining one's
lendings and borrowings to sixpences and shillings, a
request for a pound comes as something of a blow.

"What on earth for?" asked Mike.

"I say, do you mind if I don't tell you? I don't want to
tell anybody. The fact is, I'm in a beastly hole."

"Oh, sorry," said Mike. "As a matter of fact, I do
happen to have a quid. You can freeze on to it, if you like.
But it's about all I have got, so don't be shy about paying it
back."

Jellicoe was profuse in his thanks, and disappeared in a
cloud of gratitude.

Mike felt that Fate was treating him badly. Being kept
in on Saturday meant that he would be unable to turn out
for Little Borlock against Claythorpe, the return match.
In the previous game he had scored ninety-eight, and there
was a lob bowler in the Claythorpe ranks whom he was particularly anxious to meet again. Having to yield a sover-
eign to Jellicoe—why on earth did the man want all that?—
meant that, unless a carefully worded letter to his brother
Bob at Oxford had the desired effect, he would be practically
penniless for weeks.

In a gloomy frame of mind he sat down to write to Bob,
who was playing regularly for the 'Varsity this season,
and only the previous week had made a century against

63

Sussex, so might be expected to be in a sufficiently softened mood to advance the needful. (Which, it may be stated at once, he did, by return of post.)

Mike was struggling with the opening sentences of this letter—he was never a very ready writer—when Stone and Robinson burst into the room.

Mike put down his pen, and got up. He was in warlike mood, and welcomed the intrusion. If Stone and Robinson wanted battle, they should have it.

But the motives of the expedition were obviously friendly. Stone beamed. Robinson was laughing.

"You're a sportsman," said Robinson.

"What did he give you?" asked Stone.

They sat down, Robinson on the table, Stone in Psmith's deck-chair. Mike's heart warmed to them. The little disturbance in the dormitory was a thing of the past, done with, forgotten, contemporary with Julius Caesar. He felt that he, Stone and Robinson must learn to know and appreciate one another.

There was, as a matter of fact, nothing much wrong with Stone and Robinson. They were just ordinary raggers of the type found at every public school, small and large. They were absolutely free from brain. They had a certain amount of muscle, and a vast store of animal spirits. They looked on school life purely as a vehicle for ragging. The Stones and Robinsons are the swashbucklers of the school world. They go about, loud and boisterous, with a whole-hearted and cheerful indifference to other people's feelings, treading on the toes of their neighbour and shoving him off the pavement, and always with an eye wide open for any adventure. As to the kind of adventure, they are not particular so long as it promises excitement. Sometimes they go through their whole school career without accident. More often they run up against a snag in the shape of some serious-minded and muscular person, who objects to having his toes trodden on and being shoved off the pavement, and then they usually sober down, to the mutual advantage of themselves and the rest of the community.

One's opinion of this type of youth varies according to one's point of view. Small boys whom they had occasion to kick, either from pure high spirits or as a punishment for some slip from the narrow path which the ideal small boy should tread, regarded Stone and Robinson as bullies of the genuine "Eric" and "St. Winifred's" brand. Masters were rather afraid of them. Adair had a smouldering dislike for them. They were useful at cricket, but apt not to take Sedleigh as seriously as he could have wished.

As for Mike, he now found them pleasant company, and began to get out the tea-things.

"Those Fire Brigade meetings," said Stone, "are a rag. You can do what you like, and you never get more than a hundred lines."

"Don't you!" said Mike. "I got Saturday afternoon."

"What!"

"Is Wilson in too?"

"No. He got a hundred lines."

Stone and Robinson were quite concerned.

"What a beastly swindle!"

"That's because you don't play cricket. Old Downing lets you do what you like if you join the Fire Brigade and play cricket."

"'We are, above all, a keen school,'" quoted Stone. "Don't you ever play?"

"I have played a bit," said Mike.

"Well, why don't you have a shot? We aren't such flyers here. If you know one end of a bat from the other, you could get into some sort of a team. Were you at school anywhere before you came here?"

"I was at Wrykyn."

"Why on earth did you leave?" asked Stone. "Were you sacked?"

"No. My father took me away."

"Wrykyn?" said Robinson. "Are you any relation of the Jacksons there—J. W. and the others?"

"Brother."

"What!"

"Well, didn't you play at all there?"

"Yes," said Mike, "I did. I was in the team three years, and I should have been captain this year, if I'd stopped on."

There was a profound and gratifying sensation. Stone gaped, and Robinson nearly dropped his tea-cup.

Stone broke the silence.

"But I mean to say—look here! What I mean is, why aren't you playing? Why don't you play now?"

"I do. I play for a village near here. Place called Little Borlock. A man who played against Wrykyn for the Free Foresters captains them. He asked me if I'd like some games for them."

"But why not for the school?"

"Why should I? It's much better fun for the village. You don't get ordered about by Adair, for a start."

"Adair sticks on side," said Stone.

"Enough for six," agreed Robinson.

"By Jove," said Stone, "I've got an idea. My word, what a rag!"

"What's wrong now?" inquired Mike politely.

"Why, look here. Tomorrow's Mid-term Service day. It's nowhere near the middle of the term, but they always have it in the fourth week. There's chapel at half-past nine till half-past ten. Then the rest of the day's a whole holiday. There are always house matches. We're playing Downing's. Why don't you play and let's smash them?"

"By Jove, yes," said Robinson. "Why don't you? They're always sticking on side because they've won the house cup three years running. I say, do you bat or bowl?"

"Bat. Why?"

Robinson rocked on the table.

"Why, old Downing fancies himself as a bowler. "You *must* play, and knock the cover off him."

"Masters don't play in house matches, surely?"

"This isn't a real house match. Only a friendly. Downing always turns out on Mid-term Service day. I say, do play."

"Think of the rag."

"But the team's full," said Mike.

"The list isn't up yet. We'll nip across to Barnes's study, and make him alter it."

They dashed out of the room. From down the passage Mike heard yells of "*Barnes!*" the closing of a door, and a murmur of excited conversation. Then footsteps returning down the passage.

Barnes appeared, on his face the look of one who has seen visions.

"I say," he said, "is it true? Or is Stone rotting? About Wrykyn, I mean."

"Yes, I was in the team."

Barnes was an enthusiastic cricketer. He studied his *Wisden*, and he had an immense respect for Wrykyn cricket.

"Are you the M. Jackson, then, who had an average of fifty-one point nought three last year?"

"Yes."

Barnes's manner became like that of a curate talking to a bishop.

"I say," he said, "then—er—will you play against Downing's tomorrow?"

"Rather," said Mike. "Thanks awfully. Have some tea?"

CHAPTER XI

THE MATCH WITH DOWNING'S

IT is the curious instinct which prompts most people to rub a thing in that makes the lot of the average convert an unhappy one. Only the very self-controlled can refrain from improving the occasion and scoring off the convert. Most leap at the opportunity.

It was so in Mike's case. Mike was not a genuine convert, but to Mr. Downing he had the outward aspect of one. When you have been impressing upon a non-cricketing boy for nearly a month that (*a*) the school is above all a keen school, (*b*) that all members of it should play cricket, and (*c*) that by not playing cricket he is ruining his chances in this world and imperilling them in the next; and when, quite unexpectedly, you come upon this boy dressed in cricket flannels, wearing cricket boots and carrying a cricket bag, it seems only natural to assume that you have converted him, that the seeds of your eloquence have fallen on fruitful soil and sprouted.

Mr. Downing assumed it.

He was walking to the field with Adair and another member of his team when he came upon Mike.

"What!" he cried. "Our Jackson clad in suit of mail and armed for the fray!"

This was Mr. Downing's No. 2 manner—the playful.

"This is indeed Saul among the prophets. Why this sudden enthusiasm for a game which I understood that you despised? Are our opponents so reduced?"

Psmith, who was with Mike, took charge of the affair with a languid grace which had maddened hundreds in its time, and which never failed to ruffle Mr. Downing.

68

"We are, above all, sir," he said, "a keen house. Drones are not welcomed by us. We are essentially versatile. Jackson, the archæologist of yesterday becomes the cricketer of today. It is the right spirit, sir," said Psmith earnestly. "I like to see it."

"Indeed, Smith? You are not playing yourself, I notice. Your enthusiasm has bounds."

"In our house, sir, competition is fierce, and the Selection Committee unfortunately passed me over."

There were a number of pitches dotted about over the field, for there was always a touch of the London Park about it on Mid-term Service day. Adair, as captain of cricket, had naturally selected the best for his own match. It was a good wicket, Mike saw. As a matter of fact the wickets at Sedleigh were nearly always good. Adair had infected the groundsman with some of his own keenness, with the result that that once-leisurely official now found himself sometimes, with a kind of mild surprise, working really hard. At the beginning of the previous season Sedleigh had played a scratch team from a neighbouring town on a wicket which, except for the creases, was absolutely undistinguishable from the surrounding turf, and behind the pavilion after the match Adair had spoken certain home truths to the groundsman. The latter's reformation had dated from that moment.

Barnes, timidly jubilant, came up to Mike with the news that he had won the toss, and the request that Mike would go in first with him.

In stories of the "Not Really a Duffer" type, where the nervous new boy, who has been found crying in the changing-room over the photograph of his sister, contrives to get an innings in a game, nobody suspects that he is really a prodigy till he hits the Bully's first ball out of the ground for six.

With Mike it was different. There was no pitying smile on Adair's face as he started his run preparatory to sending down the first ball. Mike, on the cricket field, could not have looked anything but a cricketer if he had turned out in a tweed suit and hobnail boots. Cricketer was written all over him—in his walk, in the way he took guard, in his stand at the wicket. Adair started to bowl with the feeling that this was somebody who had more than a little knowledge of how to deal with good bowling and punish bad.

Mike started cautiously. He was more than usually anxious to make runs today, and he meant to take no risks till he could afford to do so. He had seen Adair bowl at the nets, and he knew that he was good.

The first over was a maiden, six dangerous balls beautifully played. The fieldsmen changed over.

The general interest had now settled on the match between Outwood's and Downing's. The fact in Mike's case had gone round the field, and, as several of the other games had not yet begun, quite a large crowd had collected near the pavilion to watch. Mike's masterly treatment of the opening over had impressed the spectators, and there was a popular desire to see how he would deal with Mr. Downing's slows. It was generally anticipated that he would do something special with them.

Off the first ball of the master's over a leg-bye was run.

Mike took guard.

Mr. Downing was a bowler with a style of his own. He took two short steps, two long steps, gave a jump, took three more short steps, and ended with a combination of step and jump, during which the ball emerged from behind his back and started on its slow career to the wicket. The whole business had some of the dignity of the old-fashioned minuet, subtly blended with the careless vigour of a cake-walk. The ball, when delivered, was billed to break from leg, but the programme was subject to alterations.

If the spectators had expected Mike to begin any firework effects with the first ball, they were disappointed. He played the over through with a grace worthy of his brother Joe. The last ball he turned to leg for a single.

His treatment of Adair's next over was freer. He had got a sight of the ball now. Halfway through the over a beautiful square cut forced a passage through the crowd by the pavilion, and dashed up against the rails. He drove the sixth ball past cover for three.

The crowd was now reluctantly dispersing to its own games, but it stopped as Mr. Downing started his minuet-cake-walk, in the hope that it might see something more sensational.

This time the hope was fulfilled.

The ball was well up, slow, and off the wicket on the on-side. Perhaps if it had been allowed to pitch, it might have broken in and become quite dangerous. Mike went out at it, and hit it a couple of feet from the ground. The ball dropped with a thud and a spurting of dust in the road that ran along one side of the cricket field.

It was returned on the instalment system by helpers from other games, and the bowler began his manoeuvres again. A half-volley this time. Mike slammed it back, and mid-on, whose heart was obviously not in the thing, failed to stop it.

"Get to them, Jenkins," said Mr. Downing irritably, as the ball came back from the boundary. "Get to them."

"Sir, please, sir——"

"Don't talk in the field, Jenkins."

Having had a full-pitch hit for six and a half-volley for four, there was a strong probability that Mr. Downing would pitch his next ball short.

The expected happened. The third ball was a slow long-hop, and hit the road at about the same spot where the first had landed. A howl of untuneful applause rose from the watchers in the pavilion, and Mike, with the feeling that this sort of bowling was too good to be true, waited in position for number four.

There are moments when a sort of panic seizes a bowler. This happened now with Mr. Downing. He suddenly abandoned science and ran amok. His run lost its stateliness and increased its vigour. He charged up to the wicket as a wounded buffalo sometimes charges a gun. His whole idea now was to bowl fast.

When a slow bowler starts to bowl fast, it is usually as well to be batting, if you can manage it.

By the time the over was finished, Mike's score had been increased by sixteen, and the total of his side, in addition, by three wides.

And a shrill small voice, from the neighbourhood of the pavilion, uttered with painful distinctness the words, "Take him off!"

That was how the most sensational day's cricket began that Sedleigh had known.

A description of the details of the morning's play would be monotonous. It is enough to say that they ran on much the same lines as the third and fourth overs of the match. Mr. Downing bowled one more over, off which Mike helped himself to sixteen runs, and then retired moodily to coverpoint, where, in Adair's fifth over, he missed Barnes—the first occasion since the game began on which that mild batsman had attempted to score more than a single. Scared by this escape, Outwood's captain shrank back into his shell, sat on the splice like a limpet, and, offering no more chances, was not out at lunch time with a score of eleven.

Mike had then made a hundred and three.

As Mike was taking off his pads in the pavilion, Adair came up.

"Why did you say you didn't play cricket?" he asked abruptly.

When one has been bowling the whole morning, and bowling well, without the slightest success, one is inclined to be abrupt.

Mike finished unfastening an obstinate strap. Then he looked up.

"I didn't say anything of the kind. I said I wasn't going to play here. There's a difference. As a matter of fact, I was in the Wrykyn team before I came here. Three years."

Adair was silent for a moment.

"Will you play for us against the Old Sedleighans tomorrow?" he said at length.

Mike tossed his pads into his bag and got up.

"No, thanks."

There was a silence.

"Above it, I suppose?"

"Not a bit. Not up to it. I shall want a lot of coaching at that end net of yours before I'm fit to play for Sedleigh."

There was another pause.

"Then you won't play?" asked Adair.

"I'm not keeping you, am I?" said Mike, politely.

It was remarkable what a number of members of Outwood's house appeared to cherish a personal grudge against Mr. Downing. It had been that master's somewhat injudicious practice for many years to treat his own house as a sort of Chosen People. Of all masters, the most unpopular is he who by the silent tribunal of a school is convicted of favouritism. And the dislike deepens if it is a house which he favours and not merely individuals. On occasions when boys in his own house and boys from other houses were accomplices and partners in wrongdoing, Mr. Downing distributed his thunderbolts unequally, and the school noticed it. The result was that not only he himself, but also—which was rather unfair—his house, too, had acquired a good deal of unpopularity.

The general concensus of opinion in Outwood's during the luncheon interval was that having got Downing's up a tree, they would be fools not to make the most of the situation.

Barnes's remark that he supposed, unless anything happened and wickets began to fall a bit faster, they had better think of declaring somewhere about half-past three or four, was met with a storm of opposition.

"Declare!" said Robinson. "Great Scot, what on earth are you talking about?"

"Declare!" Stone's voice was almost a wail of indignation. "I never saw such a chump."

"They'll be rather sick if we don't, won't they?" suggested Barnes.

"Sick! I should think they would," said Stone. "That's just the gay idea. Can't you see that by a miracle we've got a chance of getting a jolly good bit of our own back against those Downing's ticks? What we've got to do is to jolly well keep them in the field all day if we can, and be jolly glad it's so beastly hot. If they lose about a dozen pounds each through sweating about in the sun after Jackson's drives, perhaps they'll stick on less side about things in general in future. Besides, I want an innings against that bilge of old Downing's, if I can get it."

"So do I," said Robinson.

"If you declare, I swear I won't field. Nor will Robinson."

"Rather not."

"Well, I won't then," said Barnes unhappily. "Only you know they're rather sick already."

"Don't you worry about that," said Stone with a wide grin. "They'll be a lot sicker before we've finished."

And so it came about that that particular Mid-term Service-day match made history. Big scores had often been put up on Mid-term Service day. Games had frequently been one-sided. But it had never happened before in the annals of the school that one side, going in first early in the morning, had neither completed its innings nor declared it closed when stumps were drawn at 6.30. In no previous Sedleigh match, after a full day's play, had the pathetic words "Did not bat" been written against the whole of one of the contending teams.

These are the things which mark epochs.

Play was resumed at 2.15. For a quarter of an hour Mike was comparatively quiet. Adair, fortified by food

74

and rest, was bowling really well, and his first half-dozen overs had to be watched carefully. But the wicket was too good to give him a chance, and Mike, playing himself in again, proceeded to get to business once more. Bowlers came and went. Adair pounded away at one end with brief intervals between the attacks. Mr. Downing took a couple more overs, in one of which a horse, passing in the road, nearly had its useful life cut suddenly short. Change-bowlers of various actions and paces, each weirder and more futile than the last, tried their luck. But still the first-wicket stand continued.

The bowling of a house team is all head and no body. The first pair probably have some idea of length and break. The first-change pair are poor. And the rest, the small change, are simply the sort of things one sees in dreams after a heavy supper, or when one is out without one's gun.

Time, mercifully, generally breaks up a big stand at cricket before the field has suffered too much, and that is what happened now. At four o'clock, when the score stood at two hundred and twenty for no wicket, Barnes, greatly daring, smote lustily at a rather wide half-volley and was caught at short-slip for thirty-three. He retired blushfully to the pavilion, amidst applause, and Stone came out.

As Mike had then made a hundred and eighty-seven, it was assumed by the field, that directly he had topped his second century, the closure would be applied and their ordeal finished. There was almost a sigh of relief when frantic cheering from the crowd told that the feat had been accomplished. The fieldsmen clapped in quite an indulgent sort of way, as who should say, "Capital, capital. And now let's start *our* innings." Some even began to edge towards the pavilion.

But the next ball was bowled, and the next over, and the next after that, and still Barnes made no sign. (The conscience-stricken captain of Outwood's was, as a matter of fact, being practically held down by Robinson and other ruffians by force.)

A grey dismay settled on the field.

The bowling had now become almost unbelievably bad. Lobs were being tried, and Stone, nearly weeping with pure joy, was playing an innings of the How-to-brighten-cricket type. He had an unorthodox style, but an excellent eye, and the road at this period of the game became absolutely unsafe for pedestrians and traffic.

Mike's pace had become slower, as was only natural, but his score, too, was mounting steadily.

"This is foolery," snapped Mr. Downing, as the three hundred and fifty went up on the board. "Barnes!" he called.

There was no reply. A committee of three was at that moment engaged in sitting on Barnes's head in the first eleven changing-room, in order to correct a more than usually feverish attack of conscience.

"Barnes!"

"Please, sir," said Stone, some species of telepathy telling him what was detaining his captain. "I think Barnes must have left the field. He has probably gone over to the house to fetch something."

"This is absurd. You must declare your innings closed. The game has become a farce."

"Declare! Sir, we can't unless Barnes does. He might be awfully annoyed if we did anything like that without consulting him."

"Absurd."

"He's very touchy, sir."

"It is perfect foolery."

"I think Jenkins is just going to bowl, sir."

Mr. Downing walked moodily to his place.

In a neat wooden frame in the senior day-room at Outwood's, just above the mantelpiece, there was on view, a week later, a slip of paper.

The writing on it was as follows:

OUTWOOD'S *v.* DOWNING'S

Outwood's.　First innings.

J. P. Barnes, *c.* Hammond, *b.* Hassall	. .	33
M. Jackson, not out	.	277
W. J. Stone, not out	.	124
Extras.	.	37
Total (for one wicket) .	.	471

Downing's did not bat.

CHAPTER XII

THE SINGULAR BEHAVIOUR OF JELLICOE

OUTWOOD'S rollicked considerably that night. Mike, if he
had cared to take the part, could have been the Petted
Hero. But a cordial invitation from the senior day-room to
be the guest of the evening at about the biggest rag of the
century had been refused on the plea of fatigue. One
does not make two hundred and seventy-seven runs on a
hot day without feeling the effects, even if one has scored
mainly by the medium of boundaries; and Mike, as he lay
back in Psmith's deck-chair, felt that all he wanted was to
go to bed and stay there for a week. His hands and arms
burned as if they were red-hot, and his eyes were so tired
that he could not keep them open.

Psmith, leaning against the mantelpiece, discoursed in a
desultory way on the day's happenings—the score off Mr.
Downing, the undeniable annoyance of that battered bowler,
and the probability of his venting his annoyance on Mike
next day.

"In theory," said he, "the manly what-d'you-call-it
of cricket and all that sort of thing ought to make him
fall on your neck tomorrow and weep over you as a foeman
worthy of his steel. But I am prepared to bet a reasonable
sum that he will give no ju-jitsu exhibition of this kind.
In fact, from what I have seen of our bright little friend, I
should say that, in a small way, he will do his best to make
it distinctly hot for you, here and there."

"I don't care," murmured Mike, shifting his aching limbs
in the chair.

"In an ordinary way, I suppose, a man can put up with
having his bowling hit a little. But your performance was

78

cruelty to animals. Twenty-eight off one over, not to mention three wides, would have made Job foam at the mouth. You will probably get sacked. On the other hand, it's worth it. You have lit a candle this day which can never be blown out. You have shown the lads of the village how Comrade Downing's bowling ought to be treated. I don't suppose he'll ever take another wicket."

"He doesn't deserve to."

Psmith smoothed his hair at the glass and turned round again.

"The only blot on this day of mirth and goodwill is," he said, "the singular conduct of our friend Jellicoe. When all the place was ringing with song and merriment, Comrade Jellicoe crept to my side, and, slipping his little hand in mine, touched me for three quid."

This interested Mike, tired as he was.

"What! Three quid!"

"Three crisp, crackling quid. He wanted four."

"But the man must be living at the rate of I don't know what. It was only yesterday that he borrowed a quid from *me*!"

"He must be saving money fast. There appear to be the makings of a financier about Comrade Jellicoe. Well, I hope, when he's collected enough for his needs, he'll pay me back a bit. I'm pretty well cleaned out."

"I got some from my brother at Oxford."

"Perhaps he's saving up to get married. We may be helping towards furnishing the home. There was a Siamese prince fellow at my dame's at Eton who had four wives when he arrived, and gathered in a fifth during his first summer holidays. It was done on the correspondence system. His Prime Minister fixed it up at the other end, and sent him the glad news on a picture postcard. I think an eye ought to be kept on Comrade Jellicoe."

Mike tumbled into bed that night like a log, but he could not sleep. He ached all over. Psmith chatted for a time on human affairs in general, and then dropped gently off. Jellicoe, who appeared to be wrapped in gloom, contributed nothing to the conversation.

After Psmith had gone to sleep, Mike lay for some time running over in his mind, as the best substitute for sleep, the various points of his innings that day. He felt very hot and uncomfortable.

Just as he was wondering whether it would not be a good idea to get up and have a cold bath, a voice spoke from the darkness at his side.

"Are you asleep, Jackson?"

"Who's that?"

"Me—Jellicoe. I can't get to sleep."

"Nor can I. I'm stiff all over."

"I'll come over and sit on your bed."

There was a creaking, and then a weight descended in the neighbourhood of Mike's toes.

Jellicoe was apparently not in conversational mood. He uttered no word for quite three minutes. At the end of which time he gave a sound midway between a snort and a sigh.

"I say, Jackson!" he said.

"Yes?"

"Have you—oh, nothing."

Silence again.

"Jackson."

"Hullo?"

"I say, what would your people say if you got sacked?"

"All sorts of things. Especially my father. Why?"

"Oh, I don't know. So would mine."

"Everybody's would, I expect."

"Yes."

The bed creaked, as Jellicoe digested these great thoughts. Then he spoke again.

"It would be a jolly beastly thing to get sacked."

Mike was too tired to give his mind to the subject. He was not really listening. Jellicoe droned on in a depressed sort of way.

"You'd get home in the middle of the afternoon, I suppose, and you'd drive up to the house, and the servant would open the door, and you'd go in. They might all be out, and then you'd have to hang about, and wait; and presently you'd hear them come in, and you'd go out into the passage, and they'd say 'Hullo!'"

Jellicoe, in order to give verisimilitude, as it were, to an otherwise bald and unconvincing narrative, flung so much agitated surprise into the last word that it woke Mike from a troubled doze into which he had fallen.

"Hullo?" he said. "What's up?"

"Then you'd say, 'Hullo!' And then they'd say, 'What are you doing here?' And you'd say——"

"What on earth are you talking about?"

"About what would happen."

"Happen when?"

"When you got home. After being sacked, you know."

"Who's been sacked?" Mike's mind was still under a cloud.

"Nobody. But if you were, I meant. And then I suppose there'd be an awful row and general sickness, and all that. And then you'd be sent into a bank, or to Australia, or something."

Mike dozed off again.

"My father would be frightfully sick. My mater would be sick. My sister would be jolly sick, too. Have you got any sisters, Jackson? I say, Jackson!"

"Hullo! What's the matter? Who's that?"

"Me—Jellicoe."

"What's up?"

"I asked you if you'd got any sisters."

"Any *what*?"

"Sisters."

"Whose sisters?"

"Yours. I asked if you'd got any."

"Any what?"

"Sisters."

"What about them?"

The conversation was becoming too intricate for Jellicoe. He changed the subject.

"I say, Jackson!"

"Well?"

"I say, you don't know anyone who could lend me a pound, do you?"

"What!" cried Mike, sitting up in bed and staring through the darkness in the direction whence the numismatist's voice was proceeding. "Do *what*?"

"I say, look out. You'll wake Smith."

"Did you say you wanted someone to lend you a quid?"

"Yes," said Jellicoe eagerly. "Do you know anyone?"

Mike's head throbbed. This thing was too much. The human brain could not be expected to cope with it. Here was a youth who had borrowed a pound from one friend the day before, and three pounds from another friend that very afternoon, already looking about him for further loans. Was it a hobby, or was he saving up to buy an aeroplane?"

"What on earth do you want a pound for?"

"I don't want to tell anybody. But it's jolly serious. I shall get sacked if I don't get it."

Mike pondered.

Those who have followed Mike's career as set forth by the present historian will have realized by this time that he was a good long way from being perfect. As the Blue-Eyed Hero he would have been a rank failure. Except on the cricket field, where he was a natural genius, he was just ordinary. He resembled ninety per cent of other members of English public schools. He had some virtues and a good many defects. He was as obstinate as a mule, though people whom he liked could do as they pleased with him. He was good-natured as a general thing, but on occasion his temper could be of the worst, and had, in his childhood, been the subject of much adverse comment among his aunts. He was rigidly truthful, where the issue concerned only himself. Where it was a case of saving a friend, he was prepared to act in a manner reminiscent of an American expert witness.

He had, in addition, one good quality without any defect to balance it. He was always ready to help people. And when he set himself to do this, he was never put off by discomfort or risk. He went at the thing with a singleness of purpose that asked no questions.

Bob's postal order, which had arrived that evening, was reposing in the breast-pocket of his coat.

It was a wrench, but, if the situation was so serious with Jellicoe, it had to be done.

Two minutes later the night was being made hideous by Jellicoe's almost tearful protestations of gratitude, and the postal order had moved from one side of the dormitory to the other.

CHAPTER XIII

JELLICOE GOES ON THE SICK-LIST

MIKE woke next morning with a confused memory of having listened to a great deal of incoherent conversation from Jellicoe, and a painfully vivid recollection of handing over the bulk of his worldly wealth to him. The thought depressed him, though it seemed to please Jellicoe, for the latter carolled in a gay undertone as he dressed, till Psmith, who had a sensitive ear, asked as a favour that these farm-yard imitations might cease until he was out of the room.

There were other things to make Mike low-spirited that morning. To begin with, he was in detention, which in itself is enough to spoil a day. It was a particularly fine day, which made the matter worse. In addition to this, he had never felt stiffer in his life. It seemed to him that the creaking of his joints as he walked must be audible to everyone within a radius of several yards. Finally, there was the interview with Mr. Downing to come. That would probably be unpleasant. As Psmith had said, Mr. Downing was the sort of master who would be likely to make trouble. The great match had not been an ordinary match. Mr. Downing was a curious man in many ways, but he did not make a fuss on ordinary occasions when his bowling proved expensive. Yesterday's performance, however, stood in a class by itself. It stood forth without disguise as a deliberate rag. One side does not keep another in the field the whole day in a one-day match except as a grisly kind of practical joke. And Mr. Downing and his house realized this. The house's way of signifying its comprehension of the fact was to be cold and distant as far as the seniors were concerned, and abusive and pugnacious as regards the juniors. Young blood had been shed overnight, and more flowed during the eleven o'clock interval that morning to avenge the insult.

Mr. Downing's methods of retaliation would have to be, of necessity, more elusive; but Mike did not doubt that in some way or other his form-master would endeavour to get a bit of his own back.

As events turned out, he was perfectly right. When a master has got his knife into a boy, especially a master who allows himself to be influenced by his likes and dislikes, he is inclined to single him out in times of stress, and savage him as if he were the official representative of the evildoers. Just as, at sea, the skipper when he has trouble with the crew, works it off on the boy.

Mr. Downing was in a sarcastic mood when he met Mike. That is to say, he began in a sarcastic strain. But this sort of thing is difficult to keep up. By the time he had reached his peroration, the rapier had given place to the bludgeon. For sarcasm to be effective, the user of it must be met half-way. His hearer must appear to be conscious of the sarcasm and moved by it. Mike, when masters waxed sarcastic towards him, always assumed an air of stolid stupidity, which was as a suit of mail against satire.

So Mr. Downing came down from the heights with a run, and began to express himself with a simple strength which it did his form good to listen to. Veterans who had been in the form for terms said afterwards that there had been nothing to touch it, in their experience of the orator, since the glorious day when Dunster, that prince of raggers, who had left at Christmas to go to a crammer's, had introduced three lively grass-snakes into the room during a Latin lesson.

"You are surrounded," concluded Mr. Downing, snapping his pencil in two in his emotion, "by an impenetrable mass of conceit and vanity and selfishness. It does not occur to you to admit your capabilities as a cricketer in an open, straightforward way and place them at the disposal of the school. No, that would not be dramatic enough for you. It would be too commonplace altogether. Far too commonplace!" Mr. Downing laughed bitterly. "No, you must conceal your capabilities. You must act a lie. You must—who is that shuffling his feet? I will not have it, I *will* have silence—you must hang back in order to make a more effective entrance, like some wretched actor who—I will *not* have this shuffling. I have spoken of this before. Macpherson, are you shuffling your feet?"

"Sir, no, sir."

"Please, sir."

"Well, Parsons?"

"I think it's the noise of the draught under the door, sir."

Instant departure of Parsons for the outer regions. And, in the excitement of this side-issue, the speaker lost his inspiration, and abruptly concluded his remarks by putting Mike on to translate in Cicero. Which Mike, who happened to have prepared the first half-page, did with much success.

The Old Boys' match was timed to begin shortly after eleven o'clock. During the interval most of the school walked across the field to look at the pitch. One or two of the Old Boys had already changed and were practising in front of the pavilion.

It was through one of these batsmen that an accident occurred which had a good deal of influence on Mike's affairs.

Mike had strolled out by himself. Halfway across the field Jellicoe joined him. Jellicoe was cheerful, and rather embarrassingly grateful. He was just in the middle of his harangue when the accident happened.

To their left, as they crossed the field, a long youth, with the faint beginnings of a moustache and a blazer that lit up the surrounding landscape like a glowing beacon, was lashing out recklessly at a friend's bowling. Already he had gone within an ace of slaying a small boy. As Mike and Jellicoe proceeded on their way, there was a shout of "Heads!"

The almost universal habit of batsmen of shouting "Heads!" at whatever height from the ground the ball may be, is not a little confusing. The average person, on hearing the shout, puts his hands over his skull, crouches down and trusts to luck. This is an excellent plan if the ball is falling, but is not much protection against a skimming drive along the ground.

When "Heads!" was called on the present occasion, Mike and Jellicoe instantly assumed the crouching attitude.

Jellicoe was the first to abandon it. He uttered a yell and sprang into the air. After which he sat down and began to nurse his ankle.

The bright-blazered youth walked up.

"Awfully sorry, you know. Hurt?"

Jellicoe was pressing the injured spot tenderly with his finger-tips, uttering sharp howls whenever, zeal out-running discretion, he prodded himself too energetically.

"Silly ass, Dunster," he groaned, "slamming about like that."

"Awfully sorry. But I did yell."

"It's swelling up rather," said Mike. "You'd better get over to the house and have it looked at. Can you walk?"

Jellicoe tried, but sat down again with a loud "Ow!" At that moment the bell rang.

"I shall have to be going in," said Mike, "or I'd have helped you over."

"I'll give you a hand," said Dunster.

He helped the sufferer to his feet and they staggered off together, Jellicoe hopping, Dunster advancing with a sort of polka step. Mike watched them start and then turned to go in.

CHAPTER XIV

MIKE RECEIVES A COMMISSION

THERE is only one thing to be said in favour of detention on a fine summer's afternoon, and that is that it is very pleasant to come out of. The sun never seems so bright or the turf so green as during the first five minutes after one has come out of the detention-room. One feels as if one were entering a new and very delightful world. There is also a touch of the Rip van Winkle feeling. Everything seems to have gone on and left one behind. Mike, as he walked to the cricket field, felt very much behind the times.

Arriving on the field he found the Old Boys batting. He stopped and watched an over of Adair's. The fifth ball bowled a man. Mike made his way towards the pavilion.

Before he got there he heard his name called, and turning, found Psmith seated under a tree with the bright-blazered Dunster.

"Return of the exile," said Psmith. "A joyful occasion tinged with melancholy. Have a cherry?—take one or two. These little acts of unremembered kindness are what one needs after a couple of hours in extra pupil-room. Restore your tissues, Comrade Jackson, and when you have finished those, apply again."

"Is your name Jackson?" inquired Dunster, "because Jellicoe wants to see you."

"Alas, poor Jellicoe!" said Psmith. "He is now prone on his bed in the dormitory—there a sheer hulk lies poor Tom Jellicoe, the darling of the crew, faithful below he did his duty, but Comrade Dunster has broached him to. I have just been hearing the melancholy details."

"Old Smith and I," said Dunster, "were at a prep school together. I'd no idea I should find him here."

"It was a wonderfully stirring sight when we met," said Psmith; "not unlike the meeting of Ulysses and the hound Argos, of whom you have doubtless read in the course of your dabblings in the classics. I was Ulysses; Dunster gave a life-like representation of the faithful dawg."

"You still jaw as much as ever, I notice," said the animal delineator, fondling the beginnings of his moustache.

"More," sighed Psmith, "more. Is anything irritating you?" he added, eyeing the other's manœuvres with interest.

"You needn't be a funny ass, man," said Dunster, pained; "heaps of people tell me I ought to have it waxed."

"What it really wants is top-dressing with guano. Hullo! another man out. Adair's bowling better to-day than he did yesterday."

"I heard about yesterday," said Dunster. "It must have been a rag! Couldn't we work off some other rag on somebody before I go? I shall be stopping here till Monday in the village. Well hit, sir—Adair's bowling is perfectly simple if you go out to it."

"Comrade Dunster went out to it first ball," said Psmith to Mike.

"Oh! chuck it, man; the sun was in my eyes. I hear Adair's got a match on with the M.C.C. at last."

"Has he?" said Psmith; "I hadn't heard. Archæology claims so much of my time that I have little leisure for listening to cricket chit-chat."

"What was it Jellicoe wanted?" asked Mike; "was it anything important?"

"He seemed to think so—he kept telling me to tell you to go and see him."

"I fear Comrade Jellicoe is a bit of a weak-minded blitherer——"

"Did you ever hear of a rag we worked off on Jellicoe once?" asked Dunster. "The man has absolutely no sense of humour—can't see when he's being rotted. Well, it was like this—Hullo! We're all out—I shall have to be going out to field again, I suppose, dash it! I'll tell you when I see you again."

"I shall count the minutes," said Psmith.

Mike stretched himself; the sun was very soothing after his two hours in the detention-room; he felt disinclined for exertion.

"I don't suppose it's anything special about Jellicoe, do you?" he said. "I mean, it'll keep till tea-time; it's no catch having to sweat across to the house now."

"Don't dream of moving," said Psmith. "I have several rather profound observations on life to make and I can't make them without an audience. Soliloquy is a knack. Hamlet had got it, but probably only after years of patient practice. Personally, I need some one to listen when I talk. I like to feel that I am doing good. You stay where you are—don't interrupt too much."

Mike tilted his hat over his eyes and abandoned Jellicoe.

It was not until the lock-up bell rang that he remembered him. He went over to the house and made his way to the dormitory, where he found the injured one in a parlous state, not so much physical as mental. The doctor had seen his ankle and reported that it would be on the active list in a couple of days. It was Jellicoe's mind that needed attention now.

Mike found him in a condition bordering on collapse.

"I say, you might have come before!" said Jellicoe.

"What's up? I didn't know there was such a hurry about it—what did you want?"

"It's no good now," said Jellicoe gloomily; "it's too late, I shall get sacked."

"What on earth are you talking about? What's the row?"

"It's about that money."

"What about it?"

"I had to pay it to a man today, or he said he'd write to the Head—then of course I should get sacked. I was going to take the money to him this afternoon, only I got crocked, so I couldn't move. I wanted to get hold of you to ask you to take it for me—it's too late now!"

Mike's face fell. "Oh, hang it!" he said, "I'm awfully sorry. I'd no idea it was anything like that—what a fool I was! Dunster did say he thought it was something important, only like an ass I thought it would do if I came over at lock-up."

"It doesn't matter," said Jellicoe miserably; "it can't be helped."

"Yes, it can," said Mike. "I know what I'll do—it's all right. I'll get out of the house after lights-out."

Jellicoe sat up. "You can't! You'd get sacked if you were caught."

"Who would catch me? There was a chap at Wrykyn I knew who used to break out every night nearly and go and pot at cats with an air-pistol; it's as easy as anything."

The toad-under-the-harrow expression began to fade from Jellicoe's face. "I say, do you think you could, really?"

"Of course I can! It'll be rather a rag."

"I say, it's frightfully decent of you."

"What absolute rot!"

"But look here, are you certain——"

"I shall be all right. Where do you want me to go?"

"It's a place about a mile or two from here, called Lower Borlock."

"Lower Borlock?"

"Yes, do you know it?"

"Rather! I've been playing cricket for them all the term."

"I say, have you? Do you know a man called Barley?"

"Barley? Rather—he runs the 'White Boar.'"

"He's the chap I owe the money to."

"Old Barley!"

Mike knew the landlord of the "White Boar" well; he was the wag of the village team. Every village team, for some mysterious reason, has its comic man. In the Lower Borlock eleven Mr. Barley filled the post. He was a large, stout man, with a red and cheerful face, who looked exactly like the jovial innkeeper of melodrama.

He was the last man Mike would have expected to do the "money by Monday-week or I write to the headmaster" business.

But he reflected that he had only seen him in his leisure moments, when he might naturally be expected to unbend and be full of the milk of human kindness. Probably in business hours he was quite different. After all, pleasure is one thing and business another.

Besides, five pounds is a large sum of money, and if Jellicoe owed it, there was nothing strange in Mr. Barley's doing everything he could to recover it.

He wondered a little what Jellicoe could have been doing to run up a bill as big as that, but it did not occur to him to ask, which was unfortunate, as it might have saved him a good deal of inconvenience. It seemed to him that it was none of his business to inquire into Jellicoe's private affairs. He took the envelope containing the money without question.

"I shall bike there, I think," he said, "if I can get into the shed."

The school's bicycles were stored in a shed by the pavilion.

"You can manage that," said Jellicoe; "it's locked up at night, but I had a key made to fit it last summer, because I used to get out in the early morning sometimes before it was opened."

"Got it on you?"

"Smith's got it."

"I'll get it from him."

"I say!"

"Well?"

"Don't tell Smith why you want it, will you? I don't want anybody to know—if a thing once starts getting about it's all over the place in no time."

"All right, I won't tell him."

"I say, thanks most awfully! I don't know what I should have done, I——"

"Oh, chuck it!" said Mike.

CHAPTER XV

AND FULFILS IT

M IKE started on his ride to Lower Borlock with mixed feelings. It is pleasant to be out on a fine night in summer, but the pleasure is to a certain extent modified when one feels that to be detected will mean expulsion.

Mike did not want to be expelled, for many reasons. Now that he had grown used to the place he was enjoying himself at Sedleigh to a certain extent. He still harboured a feeling of resentment against the school in general and Adair in particular, but it was pleasant in Outwood's now that he had got to know some of the members of the house, and he liked playing cricket for Lower Borlock; also, he was fairly certain that his father would not let him go to Cambridge if he were expelled from Sedleigh. Mr. Jackson was easy-going with his family, but occasionally his foot came down like a steam hammer, as witness the Wrykyn school report affair.

So Mike pedalled along rapidly, being wishful to get the job done without delay.

Psmith had yielded up the key, but his inquiries as to why it was needed had been embarrassing. Mike's statement that he wanted to get up early and have a ride had been received by Psmith, with whom early rising was not a hobby, with honest amazement and a flood of advice and warning on the subject.

"One of the Georges," said Psmith, "I forget which, once said that a certain number of hours' sleep a day— I cannot recall for the moment how many—made a man something, which for the time being has slipped my memory. However, there you are. I've given you the main idea of the thing; and a German doctor says that early rising causes insanity. Still, if you're bent on it——" After which he had handed over the key.

Mike wished he could have taken Psmith into his confidence. Probably he would have volunteered to come, too; Mike would have been glad of a companion.

It did not take him long to reach Lower Borlock. The "White Boar" stood at the far end of the village, by the cricket field. He rode past the church—standing out black and mysterious against the light sky—and the rows of silent cottages, until he came to the inn.

The place was shut, of course, and all the lights were out —it was some time past eleven.

The advantage an inn has over a private house, from the point of view of the person who wants to get into it when it has been locked up, is that a nocturnal visit is not so unexpected in the case of the former. Preparations have been made to meet such an emergency. Where with a private house you would probably have to wander round heaving rocks and end by climbing up a water-spout, when you want to get into an inn you simply ring the night-bell, which, communicating with the boots' room, has that hard-worked menial up and doing in no time.

After Mike had waited for a few minutes there was a rattling of chains and a shooting of bolts and the door opened.

"Yes, sir?" said the boots, appearing in his shirt-sleeves. "Why, 'ullo! Mr. Jackson, sir!"

Mike was well known to all dwellers in Lower Borlock, his scores being the chief topic of conversation when the day's labours were over.

"I want to see Mr. Barley, Jack."

"He's bin' in bed this half-hour back, Mr. Jackson."

"I must see him. Can you get him down?"

The boots looked doubtful. "Roust the guv'nor outer bed?" he said.

Mike quite admitted the gravity of the task. The landlord of the "White Boar" was one of those men who need a beauty sleep.

94

"I wish you would—it's a thing that can't wait. I've got some money to give to him."

"Oh, if it's *that*——" said the boots.

Five minutes later mine host appeared in person, looking more than usually portly in a check dressing-gown and red bedroom slippers.

"You can pop off, Jack."

Exit boots to his slumbers once more.

"Well, Mr. Jackson, what's it all about?"

"Jellicoe asked me to come and bring you the money."

"The money? What money?"

"What he owes you; the five pounds, of course."

"The five——" Mr. Barley stared open mouthed at Mike for a moment; then he broke into a roar of laughter which shook the sporting prints on the wall and drew barks from dogs in some distant part of the house. He staggered about laughing and coughing till Mike began to expect a fit of some kind. Then he collapsed into a chair, which creaked under him, and wiped his eyes.

"Oh dear!" he said, "oh dear! The five pounds!"

Mike was not always abreast of the rustic idea of humour, and now he felt particularly fogged. For the life of him he could not see what there was to amuse anyone so much in the fact that a person who owed five pounds was ready to pay it back. It was an occasion for rejoicing, perhaps, but rather for a solemn, thankful, eyes-raised-to-heaven kind of rejoicing.

"What's up?" he asked.

"Five pounds!"

"You might tell us the joke."

Mr. Barley opened the letter, read it, and had another attack; when this was finished he handed the letter to Mike, who was waiting patiently by, hoping for light, and requested him to read it.

"Dear, dear!" chuckled Mr. Barley, "five pounds! They may teach you young gentlemen to talk Latin and Greek and what not at your school, but it 'ud do a lot more good if they'd teach you how many beans make five; it 'ud

do a lot more good if they'd teach you to come in when it
rained; it 'ud do——"

Mike was reading the letter.

"Dear Mr. Barley," it ran.
"I send the £5, which I could not get before. I hope it is in
time, because I don't want you to write to the headmaster.
I am sorry Jane and John ate your wife's hat and the chicken
and broke the vase."

There was some more to the same effect; it was signed
"T. G. Jellicoe."

"What on earth's it all about?" said Mike, finishing this
curious document.

Mr. Barley slapped his leg. "Why, Mr. Jellicoe keeps
two dogs here; I keep 'em for him till the young gentlemen
go home for their holidays. Aberdeen terriers, they are,
and as sharp as mustard. Mischief! I believe you, but,
love us! they don't do no harm! Bite up an old shoe
sometimes and such sort of things. The other day, last
Wednesday it were, about 'ar parse five, Jane—she's the
worst of the two, always up to it, she is—she got hold of
my old hat and had it in bits before you could say knife.
John upset a china vase in one of the bedrooms chasing a
mouse, and they got on the coffee-room table and ate half a
cold chicken what had been left there. So I says to myself,
'I'll have a game with Mr. Jellicoe over this,' and I sits
down and writes off saying the little dogs have eaten a
valuable hat and a chicken and what not, and the damage'll
be five pounds, and will he kindly remit same by Saturday
night at the latest or I write to his headmaster. Love us!"
Mr. Barley slapped his thigh, "he took it all in, every word
—and here's the five pounds in cash in this envelope here!
I haven't had such a laugh since we got old Tom Raxley
out of bed at twelve of a winter's night by telling him his
house was a-fire."

It is not always easy to appreciate a joke of the practical
order if one has been made even merely part victim of it.
Mike, as he reflected that he had been dragged out of his

house in the middle of the night, in contravention of all school rules and discipline, simply in order to satisfy Mr. Barley's sense of humour, was more inclined to be abusive than mirthful. Running risks is all very well when they are necessary, or if one chooses to run them for one's own amusement, but to be placed in a dangerous position, a position imperilling one's chance of going to the 'Varsity, is another matter altogether.

But it is impossible to abuse the Barley type of man. Barley's enjoyment of the whole thing was so honest and child-like. Probably it had given him the happiest quarter of an hour he had known for years, since, in fact, the affair of old Tom Raxley. It would have been cruel to damp the man.

So Mike laughed perfunctorily, took back the envelope with the five pounds, accepted a ginger-beer and a plateful of biscuits, and rode off on his return journey.

Mention has been made above of the difference which exists between getting into an inn after lock-up and into a private house. Mike was to find this out for himself.

His first act on arriving at Sedleigh was to replace his bicycle in the shed. This he accomplished with success. It was pitch-dark in the shed, and as he wheeled his machine in, his foot touched something on the floor. Without waiting to discover what this might be, he leaned his bicycle against the wall, went out, and locked the door, after which he ran across to Outwood's.

Fortune had favoured his undertaking by decreeing that a stout drain-pipe should pass up the wall within a few inches of his and Psmith's study. On the first day of term, it may be remembered he had wrenched away the wooden bar which bisected the window-frame, thus rendering exit and entrance almost as simple as they had been for Wyatt during Mike's first term at Wrykyn.

He proceeded to scale this water-pipe.

He had got about halfway up when a voice from somewhere below cried, "Who's that?"

CHAPTER XVI

PURSUIT

THESE things are Life's Little Difficulties. One can
never tell precisely how one will act in a sudden emergency. The right thing for Mike to have done at this crisis
was to have ignored the voice, carried on up the water-
pipe, and through the study window, and gone to bed.
It was extremely unlikely that anybody could have recognized him at night against the dark background of the
house. The position then would have been that somebody
in Mr. Outwood's house had been seen breaking in after
lights-out; but it would have been very difficult for the
authorities to have narrowed the search down any further
than that. There were thirty-four boys in Outwood's, of
whom about fourteen were much the same size and build as
Mike.

The suddenness, however, of the call caused Mike to
lose his head. He made the strategic error of sliding
rapidly down the pipe, and running.

There were two gates to Mr. Outwood's front garden.
The drive ran in a semi-circle, of which the house was the
centre. It was from the right-hand gate, nearest to Mr.
Downing's house, that the voice had come, and, as Mike
came to the ground, he saw a stout figure galloping towards
him from that direction. He bolted like a rabbit for the
other gate. As he did so, his pursuer again gave tongue.

"Oo-oo-oo yer!" was the exact remark.

Whereby Mike recognized him as the school sergeant.
"Oo-oo-oo yer!" was that militant gentleman's habitual
way of beginning a conversation.

With this knowledge, Mike felt easier in his mind. Sergeant Collard was a man of many fine qualities (notably a talent for what he was wont to call "spott'n," a mysterious gift which he exercised on the rifle range), but he could not run. There had been a time in his hot youth when he had sprinted like an untamed mustang in pursuit of volatile Pathans in Indian hill wars, but Time, increasing his girth, had taken from him the taste for such exercise. When he moved now it was at a stately walk. The fact that he ran tonight showed how the excitement of the chase had entered into his blood.

"Oo-oo-oo yer!" he shouted again, as Mike, passing through the gate, turned into the road that led to the school. Mike's attentive ear noted that the bright speech was a shade more puffily delivered this time. He began to feel that this was not such bad fun after all. He would have liked to be in bed, but, if that was out of the question, this was certainly the next best thing.

He ran on, taking things easily, with the sergeant panting in his wake, till he reached the entrance to the school grounds. He dashed in and took cover behind a tree.

Presently the sergeant turned the corner, going badly and evidently cured of a good deal of the fever of the chase. Mike heard him toil on for a few yards and then stop. A sound of panting was borne to him.

Then the sound of footsteps returning, this time at a walk. They passed the gate and went on down the road.

The pursuer had given the thing up.

Mike waited for several minutes behind his tree. His programme now was simple. He would give Sergeant Collard about half an hour, in case the latter took it into his head to "guard home" by waiting at the gate. Then he would trot softly back, shoot up the water-pipe once more, and so to bed. It had just struck a quarter to something —twelve, he supposed—on the school clock. He would wait till a quarter past.

Meanwhile, there was nothing to be gained from lurking behind a tree. He left his cover, and started to stroll in the

99

direction of the pavilion. Having arrived there, he sat on the steps, looking out on to the cricket field.

His thoughts were miles away, at Wrykyn, when he was recalled to Sedleigh by the sound of somebody running. Focusing his gaze, he saw a dim figure moving rapidly across the cricket field straight for him.

His first impression, that he had been seen and followed, disappeared as the runner, instead of making for the pavilion, turned aside, and stopped at the door of the bicycle shed. Like Mike, he was evidently possessed of a key, for Mike heard it grate in the lock. At this point he left the pavilion and hailed his fellow rambler by night in a cautious undertone.

The other appeared startled.

"Who the dickens is that?" he asked. "Is that you, Jackson?"

Mike recognized Adair's voice. The last person he would have expected to meet at midnight obviously on the point of going for a bicycle ride.

"What are you doing out here, Jackson?"

"What are you, if it comes to that?"

Adair was adjusting his front light.

"I'm going for the doctor. One of the chaps in our house is bad."

"Oh!"

"What are you doing out here?"

"Just been for a stroll."

"Hadn't you better be getting back?"

"Plenty of time."

"I suppose you think you're doing something tremendously brave and dashing?"

"Hadn't you better be going to the doctor?"

"If you want to know what I think——"

"I don't. So long."

Mike turned away, whistling between his teeth. After a moment's pause, Adair rode off. Mike saw his light pass across the field and through the gate. The school clock struck the quarter.

It seemed to Mike that Sergeant Collard, even if he had started to wait for him at the house, would not keep up the vigil for more than half an hour. He would be safe now in trying for home again.

He walked in that direction.

Now it happened that Mr. Downing, aroused from his first sleep by the news, conveyed to him by Adair, that MacPhee, one of the junior members of Adair's dormitory, was groaning and exhibiting other symptoms of acute illness, was disturbed in his mind. Most house-masters feel uneasy in the event of illness in their houses, and Mr. Downing was apt to get jumpy beyond the ordinary on such occasions. All that was wrong with MacPhee, as a matter of fact, was a very fair stomachache, the direct and legitimate result of eating six buns, half a coconut, three doughnuts, two ices, an apple, and a pound of cherries, and washing the lot down with tea. But Mr. Downing saw in his attack the beginnings of some deadly scourge which would sweep through and decimate the house. He had despatched Adair for the doctor, and, after spending a few minutes prowling restlessly about his room, was now standing at his front gate, waiting for Adair's return.

It came about, therefore, that Mike, sprinting lightly in the direction of home and safety, had his already shaken nerves further maltreated by being hailed, at a range of about two yards, with a cry of "Is that you, Adair?" The next moment Mr. Downing emerged from his gate.

Mike stood not upon the order of his going. He was off like an arrow—a flying figure of Guilt. Mr. Downing, after the first surprise, seemed to grasp the situation. Ejaculating at intervals the words, "Who is that? Stop! Who is that? Stop!" he dashed after the much-enduring Wrykynian at an extremely creditable rate of speed. Mr. Downing was by way of being a sprinter. He had won handicap events at College sports at Oxford, and, if Mike had not got such a good start, the race might have been over in the first fifty yards. As it was, that victim of Fate, going well, kept ahead. At the entrance to the school grounds he led by a dozen yards. The procession passed into the field, Mike heading as before for the pavilion.

As they raced across the soft turf, an idea occurred to Mike which he was accustomed in after years to attribute to genius, the one flash of it which had ever illumined his life.

It was this.

One of Mr. Downing's first acts, on starting the Fire Brigade at Sedleigh, had been to institute an alarm bell. It had been rubbed into the school officially—in speeches from the dais—by the headmaster, and unofficially—in earnest private conversations—by Mr. Downing, that at the sound of this bell, at whatever hour of day or night, every member of the school must leave his house in the quickest possible way, and make for the open. The bell might mean that the school was on fire, or it might mean that one of the houses was on fire. In any case, the school had its orders—to get out into the open at once.

Nor must it be supposed that the school was without practice at this feat. Every now and then a notice would be found posted up on the board to the effect that there would be fire drill during the dinner hour that day. Some-- times the performance was bright and interesting, as on the occasion when Mr. Downing, marshalling the brigade at his front gate, had said, "My house is supposed to be on fire. Now let's do a record!" which the Brigade, headed by Stone and Robinson, obligingly did. They fastened the hose to the hydrant, smashed a window on the ground floor (Mr. Downing having retired for a moment to talk with the headmaster), and poured a stream of water into the room. When Mr. Downing was at liberty to turn his attention to the matter, he found that the room selected was his private study, most of the light furniture of which was floating on a miniature lake. That episode had rather discouraged his passion for realism, and fire drill since then had taken the form, for the most part, of "practising escaping." This was done by means of canvas chutes, kept in the dormitories. At the sound of the bell the prefect of the dormitory would heave one end of the chute out of window, the other end being fastened to the sill. He would then go down it himself, using his elbows as a brake. Then the second man would follow his example, and these two, standing below, would hold the end of the chute so that the rest of the dormitory could fly rapidly down it without injury, except to their digestions.

After the first novelty of the thing had worn off, the school had taken a rooted dislike to fire drill. It was a matter for self-congratulation among them that Mr. Downing had never been able to induce the headmaster to allow the alarm bell to be sounded for fire drill at night. The headmaster, a man who had his views on the amount of sleep necessary for the growing boy, had drawn the line at night operations. "Sufficient unto the day" had been the gist of his reply. If the alarm bell were to ring at night when there was no fire, the school might mistake a genuine alarm of fire for a bogus one, and refuse to hurry themselves.

So Mr. Downing had had to be content with day drill.

The alarm bell hung in the archway, leading into the school grounds. The end of the rope, when not in use, was fastened to a hook halfway up the wall.

Mike, as he raced over the cricket field, made up his mind in a flash that his only chance of getting out of this tangle was to shake his pursuer off for a space of time long enough to enable him to get to the rope and tug it. Then the school would come out. He would mix with them, and in the subsequent confusion get back to bed unnoticed.

The task was easier than it would have seemed at the beginning of the chase. Mr. Downing, owing to the two facts that he was not in the strictest training, and that it is only a Bannister who can run for any length of time at top speed shouting "Who is that? Stop! Who is that? Stop!" was beginning to feel distressed. There were bellows to mend in the Downing camp. Mike perceived this, and forced the pace. He rounded the pavilion ten yards to the good. Then, heading for the gate, he put all he knew into one last sprint. Mr. Downing was not equal to the effort. He worked gamely for a few strides, then fell behind. When Mike reached the gate, a good forty yards separated them.

As far as Mike could judge—he was not in a condition to make nice calculations—he had about four seconds in which to get busy with that bell rope.

Probably nobody has ever crammed more energetic work into four seconds than he did then.

The night was as still as only an English summer night can be, and the first clang of the clapper sounded like a million iron girders falling from a height on to a sheet of tin. He tugged away furiously, with an eye on the now rapidly advancing and loudly shouting figure of the house-master.

And from the darkened house beyond there came a gradually swelling hum, as if a vast hive of bees had been disturbed.

The school was awake.

CHAPTER XVII

THE DECORATION OF SAMMY

Psmith leaned against the mantelpiece in the senior day-room at Outwood's—since Mike's innings against Downing's the Lost Lambs had been received as brothers by that centre of disorder, so that even Spiller was compelled to look on the hatchet as buried—and gave his views on the events of the preceding night, or, rather, of that morning, for it was nearer one than twelve when peace had once more fallen on the school.

"Nothing that happens in this loony bin," said Psmith, "has power to surprise me now. There was a time when I might have thought it a little unusual to have to leave the house through a canvas chute at one o'clock in the morning, but I suppose it's quite the regular thing here. Old school tradition, &c Men leave the school, and find that they've got so accustomed to jumping out of windows that they look on it as a sort of affectation to go out by the door. I suppose none of you merchants can give me any idea when the next knock-about entertainment of this kind is likely to take place?"

"I wonder who rang that bell!" said Stone. "Jolly sporting idea."

"I believe it was Downing himself. If it was, I hope he's satisfied."

Jellicoe, who was appearing in society supported by a stick, looked meaningly at Mike, and giggled, receiving in answer a stony stare. Mike had informed Jellicoe of the details of his interview with Mr. Barley at the "White Boar," and Jellicoe, after a momentary splutter of wrath against the practical joker, was now in a particular light-hearted mood. He hobbled about, giggling at nothing and at peace with all the world.

"It was a stirring scene," said Psmith. "The agility with which Comrade Jellicoe boosted himself down the chute was a triumph of mind over matter. He seemed to forget his ankle. It was the nearest thing to a Boneless Acrobatic Wonder that I have ever seen."

"I was in a beastly funk, I can tell you."

Stone gurgled.

"So was I," he said, "for a bit. Then, when I saw that it was all a rag, I began to look about for ways of doing the thing really well. I emptied about six jugs of water on a gang of kids under my window."

"I rushed into Downing's, and ragged some of the beds," said Robinson.

"It was an invigorating time," said Psmith. "A sort of pageant. I was particularly struck with the way some of the bright lads caught hold of the idea. There was no skimping. Some of the kids, to my certain knowledge, went down the chute a dozen times. There's nothing like doing a thing thoroughly. I saw them come down, rush upstairs, and be saved again, time after time. The thing became chronic with them. I should say Comrade Downing ought to be satisfied with the high state of efficiency to which he has brought us. At any rate I hope——"

There was a sound of hurried footsteps outside the door, and Sharpe, a member of the senior day-room, burst excitedly in. He seemed amused.

"I say, have you chaps seen Sammy?"

"Seen who?" said Stone. "Sammy? Why?"

"You'll know in a second. He's just outside. Here, Sammy, Sammy, Sammy! Sam! Sam!"

A bark and a patter of feet outside.

"Come on, Sammy. Good dog."

There was a moment's silence. Then a great yell of laughter burst forth. Even Psmith's massive calm was shattered. As for Jellicoe, he sobbed in a corner.

Sammy's beautiful white coat was almost entirely concealed by a thick covering of bright red paint. His head, with the exception of the ears, was untouched, and his serious, friendly eyes seemed to emphasise the weirdness of his appearance. He stood in the doorway, barking and wagging his tail, plainly puzzled at his reception. He was a popular dog, and was always well received when he visited any of the houses, but he had never before met with enthusiasm like this.

"Good old Sammy!"

"What on earth's been happening to him?"

"Who did it?"

Sharpe, the introducer, had no views on the matter.

"I found him outside Downing's, with a crowd round him. Everybody seems to have seen him. I wonder who on earth has gone and mucked him up like that!"

Mike was the first to show any sympathy for the mal-treated animal.

"Poor old Sammy," he said, kneeling on the floor beside the victim, and scratching him under the ear. "What a beastly shame! It'll take hours to wash all that off him, and he'll hate it."

"It seems to me," said Psmith, regarding Sammy dispassionately through his eyeglass, "that it's not a case for mere washing. They'll either have to skin him bodily, or leave the thing to time. Time, the Great Healer. In a year or two he'll fade to a delicate pink. I don't see why you shouldn't have a pink bull-terrier. It would lend a touch of distinction to the place. Crowds would come in excursion trains to see him. By charging a small fee you might make him self-supporting. I think I'll suggest it to Comrade Downing."

"There'll be a row about this," said Stone.

"Rows are rather sport when you're not mixed up in them," said Robinson, philosophically. "There'll be another if we don't start off for chapel soon. It's a quarter to."

There was a general move. Mike was the last to leave the room. As he was going, Jellicoe stopped him. Jellicoe was staying in that Sunday, owing to his ankle.

"I say," said Jellicoe, "I just wanted to thank you again about that——"

"Oh, that's all right."

"No, but it really was awfully decent of you. You might have got into a frightful row. Were you nearly caught?"

"Jolly nearly."

"It *was* you who rang the bell, wasn't it?"

"Yes, it was. But for goodness' sake don't go gassing about it, or somebody will get to hear who oughtn't to, and I shall be sacked."

"All right. But, I say, you *are* a chap!"

"What's the matter now?"

"I mean about Sammy, you know. It's a jolly good score off old Downing. He'll be frightfully sick."

"Sammy!" cried Mike. "My good man, you don't think I did that, do you? What absolute rot! I never touched the poor brute."

"Oh, all right," said Jellicoe. "But I wasn't going to tell anyone, of course."

"What do you mean?"

"You *are* a chap!" giggled Jellicoe.

Mike walked to chapel rather thoughtfully.

CHAPTER XVIII

MR. DOWNING ON THE SCENT

THERE was just one moment, the moment in which, on going down to the junior day-room of his house to quell an unseemly disturbance, he was boisterously greeted by a vermilion bull-terrier, when Mr. Downing was seized with a hideous fear lest he had lost his senses. Glaring down at the crimson animal that was pawing at his knees, he clutched at his reason for one second as a drowning man clutches at a lifebelt.

Then the happy laughter of the young onlookers re-assured him.

"Who——" he shouted, "WHO has done this?"

"Please, sir, we don't know," shrilled the chorus.

"Please, sir, he came in like that."

"Please, sir, we were sitting here when he suddenly ran in, all red."

A voice from the crowd: "Look at old Sammy!"

The situation was impossible. There was nothing to be done. He could not find out by verbal inquiry who had painted the dog. The possibility of Sammy being painted red during the night had never occurred to Mr. Downing, and now that the thing had happened he had no scheme of action. As Psmith would have said, he had confused the unusual with the impossible, and the result was that he was taken by surprise.

While he was pondering on this the situation was rendered still more difficult by Sammy, who, taking advantage of the door being open, escaped and rushed into the road, thus publishing his condition to all and sundry. You can hush up a painted dog while it confines itself to your own premises, but once it has mixed with the great public this becomes out of the question. Sammy's state advanced from a private trouble into a row. Mr. Downing's next move was in the same direction that Sammy had taken, only, instead of running about the road, he went straight to the headmaster.

The Head, who had had to leave his house in the small hours in his pyjamas and a dressing-gown, was not in the best of tempers. He had a cold in the head, and also a rooted conviction that Mr. Downing, in spite of his strict orders, had rung the bell himself on the previous night in order to test the efficiency of the school in saving themselves in the event of fire. He received the house-master frostily, but thawed as the latter related the events which had led up to the ringing of the bell.

"Dear me!" he said, deeply interested. "One of the boys at the school, you think?"

"I am certain of it," said Mr. Downing.

"Was he wearing a school cap?"

"He was bare-headed. A boy who breaks out of his house at night would hardly run the risk of wearing a distinguishing cap."

"No, no, I suppose not. A big boy, you say?"

"Very big."

"You did not see his face?"

"It was dark and he never looked back—he was in front of me all the time."

"Dear me!"

"There is another matter——"

"Yes?"

"This boy, whoever he was, had done something before he rang the bell—he had painted my dog Sampson red."

The headmaster's eyes protruded from their sockets. "He—he—*what*, Mr. Downing?"

"He painted my dog red—bright red." Mr. Downing was too angry to see anything humorous to the incident. Since the previous night he had been wounded in his tenderest feelings. His Fire Brigade system had been most shamefully abused by being turned into a mere instrument in the hands of a malefactor for escaping justice, and his dog had been held up to ridicule to all the world. He did not want to smile, he wanted revenge.

The headmaster, on the other hand, did want to smile. It was not his dog, he could look on the affair with an unbiased eye, and to him there was something ludicrous in a white dog suddenly appearing as a red dog.

"It is a scandalous thing!" said Mr. Downing.

"Quite so! Quite so!" said the headmaster hastily. "I shall punish the boy who did it most severely. I will speak to the school in the Hall after chapel."

Which he did, but without result. A cordial invitation to the criminal to come forward and be executed was received in wooden silence by the school, with the exception of Johnson III, of Outwood's, who, suddenly reminded of Sammy's appearance by the headmaster's words, broke into a wild screech of laughter, and was instantly awarded two hundred lines.

The school filed out of the Hall to their various lunches, and Mr. Downing was left with the conviction that, if he wanted the criminal discovered, he would have to discover him for himself.

The great thing in affairs of this kind is to get a good start, and Fate, feeling perhaps that it had been a little hard upon Mr. Downing, gave him a most magnificent start. Instead of having to hunt for a needle in a haystack, he found himself in a moment in the position of being set to find it in a mere truss of straw.

It was Mr. Outwood who helped him. Sergeant Collard had waylaid the archæological expert on his way to chapel, and informed him that at close on twelve the night before he had observed a youth, unidentified, attempting to get into his house *via* the water-pipe. Mr. Outwood, whose thoughts were occupied with apses and plinths, not to mention cromlechs, at the time, thanked the sergeant with absent-minded politeness and passed on. Later he remembered the fact *a propos* of some reflections on the subject of burglars in mediæval England, and passed it on to Mr. Downing as they walked back to lunch.

"Then the boy was in your house!" exclaimed Mr. Downing.

"Not actually in, as far as I understand. I gather from the sergeant that he interrupted him before——"

"I mean he must have been one of the boys in your house."

"But what was he doing out at that hour?"

"He had broken out."

"Impossible, I think. Oh yes, quite impossible! I went round the dormitories as usual at eleven o'clock last night, and all the boys were asleep—all of them."

Mr. Downing was not listening. He was in a state of suppressed excitement and exultation which made it hard for him to attend to his colleague's slow utterances. He had a clue! Now that the search had narrowed itself down to Outwood's house, the rest was comparatively easy. Perhaps Sergeant Collard had actually recognized the boy. On reflection he dismissed this as unlikely, for the sergeant would scarcely have kept a thing like that to himself; but he might very well have seen more of him than he, Downing, had seen. It was only with an effort that he could keep himself from rushing to the sergeant then and there, and leaving the house lunch to look after itself. He resolved to go the moment that meal was at an end.

Sunday lunch at a public-school house is probably one of the longest functions in existence. It drags its slow length along like a languid snake, but it finishes in time. In due course Mr. Downing, after sitting still and eyeing with acute dislike everybody who asked for a second helping, found himself at liberty.

Regardless of the claims of digestion, he rushed forth on the trail.

Sergeant Collard lived with his wife and a family of unknown dimensions in the lodge at the school front gate.

Dinner was just over when Mr. Downing arrived, as a blind man could have told.

The sergeant received his visitor with dignity, ejecting the family, who were torpid after roast beef and resented having to move, in order to ensure privacy.

Having requested his host to smoke, which the latter was about to do unasked, Mr. Downing stated his case.

"Mr. Outwood," he said, "tells me that last night, sergeant, you saw a boy endeavouring to enter his house."

The sergeant blew a cloud of smoke. "Oo-oo-oo, yer," he said; "I did, sir—spotted 'im, I did. Feeflee good at spottin', I am, sir. Dook of Connaught, he used to say, ''Ere comes Sergeant Collard,' he used to say, ''e's feeflee good at spottin'.'"

"What did you do?"

"Do? Oo-oo-oo! I shouts 'Oo-oo-oo yer, yer young monkey, what yer doin' there?"

"Yes?"

"But 'e was off in a flash, and I doubles after 'im prompt."

"But you didn't catch him?"

"No, sir," admitted the sergeant reluctantly.

"Did you catch sight of his face, sergeant?"

"No, sir, 'e was doublin' away in the opposite direction."

"Did you notice anything at all about his appearance?"

"'E was a long young chap, sir, with a pair of legs on him—feeflee fast 'e run, sir. Oo-oo-oo, feeflee!"

"You noticed nothing else?"

"'E wasn't wearing no cap of any sort, sir."

"Ah!"

"Bare-'eaded, sir," added the sergeant, rubbing the point in.

"It was undoubtedly the same boy, undoubtedly! I wish you could have caught a glimpse of his face, sergeant."

"So do I, sir."

"You would not be able to recognize him again if you saw him, you think?"

"Oo-oo-oo! Wouldn't go so far as to say that, sir, 'cos yer see, I'm feeflee good at spottin', but it was a dark night."

Mr. Downing rose to go.

"Well," he said, "the search is now considerably narrowed down, considerably! If is certain that the boy was one of the boys in Mr. Outwood's house."

"Young monkeys!" interjected the sergeant helpfully.

"Good-afternoon, sergeant."

"Good afternoon to you, sir."

"Pray do not move, sergeant."

The sergeant had not shown the slightest inclination of doing anything of the kind.

"I will find my way out. Very hot today, is it not?"

"Feeflee warm, sir; weather's goin' to break' workin' up for thunder."

"I hope not. The school plays the M.C.C. on Wednesday, and it would be a pity if rain were to spoil our first fixture with them. Good afternoon."

And Mr. Downing went out into the baking sunlight, while Sergeant Collard, having requested Mrs. Collard to take the children out for a walk at once, and furthermore to give young Ernie a clip side of the 'ead, if he persisted in making so much noise, put a handkerchief over his face, rested his feet on the table, and slept the sleep of the just.

CHAPTER XIX

THE SLEUTH-HOUND

For the Doctor Watsons of this world, as opposed to the Sherlock Holmeses, success in the province of detective work must be, to a very large extent, the result of luck. Sherlock Holmes can extract a clue from a wisp of straw or a flake of cigar-ash. But Doctor Watson has got to have it taken out for him, and dusted, and exhibited clearly, with a label attached.

The average man is a Doctor Watson. We are wont to scoff in a patronizing manner at that humbler follower of the great investigator, but, as a matter of fact, we should have been just as dull ourselves. We should not even have risen to the modest level of a Scotland Yard bungler. We should simply have hung around, saying: "My dear Holmes, how——?" and all the rest of it, just as the down-trodden medico did.

It is not often that the ordinary person has any need to see what he can do in the way of detection. He gets along very comfortably in the humdrum round of life without having to measure footprints and smile quiet, tight-lipped smiles. But if ever the emergency does arise, he thinks naturally of Sherlock Holmes, and his methods.

Mr. Downing had read all the Holmes stories with great attention, and had thought many times what an incompetent ass Doctor Watson was; but, now that he had started to handle his own first case, he was compelled to admit that there was a good deal to be said in extenuation of Watson's inability to unravel tangles. It certainly was uncommonly hard, he thought, as he paced the cricket field after leaving Sergeant Collard, to detect anybody, unless you knew who had really done the crime. As he brooded over the case in hand, his sympathy for Doctor Watson increased with every minute, and he began to feel a certain resentment against Sir Arthur Conan Doyle. It was all very well for Sir Arthur to be so shrewd and infallible about tracing a mystery to its source, but he knew perfectly well who had done the thing before he started!

Now that he began really to look into this matter of the alarm bell and the painting of Sammy, the conviction was creeping over him that the problem was more difficult than a casual observer might imagine. He had got as far as finding that his quarry of the previous night was a boy in Mr. Outwood's house, but how was he to get any further? That was the thing. There was, of course, only a limited number of boys in Mr. Outwood's house as tall as the one he had pursued; but even if there had been only one other, it would have complicated matters. If you go to a boy and say, "Either you or Jones were out of your house last night at twelve o'clock," the boy does not reply, "Sir, I cannot tell a lie—I was out of my house last night at twelve o'clock." He simply assumes the animated expression of a stuffed fish, and leaves the next move to you. It is practically stalemate.

All these things passed through Mr. Downing's mind as he walked up and down the cricket field that afternoon.

What he wanted was a clue. But it is so hard for the novice to tell what is a clue and what isn't. Probably, if he only knew, there were clues lying all over the place, shouting to him to pick them up.

What with the oppressive heat of the day and the fatigue of hard-thinking, Mr. Downing was working up for a brainstorm, when Fate once more intervened, this time in the shape of Riglett, a junior member of his house.

Riglett slunk up in the shamefaced way peculiar to some boys, even when they have done nothing wrong, and, having "capped" Mr. Downing with the air of one who had been caught in the act of doing something particularly

shady, requested that he might be allowed to fetch his
bicycle from the shed.

"Your bicycle?" snapped Mr. Downing.   Much thinking had made him irritable.   "What do you want with your
bicycle?"

Riglett shuffled, stood first on his left foot, then on his
right, blushed, and finally remarked, as if it were not so
much a sound reason as a sort of feeble excuse for the low
and blackguardly fact that he wanted his bicycle, that he had
got leave for tea that afternoon.

Then Mr. Downing remembered.   Riglett had an aunt
resident about three miles from the school, whom he was
accustomed to visit occasionally on Sunday afternoons
during the term.

He felt for his bunch of keys, and made his way to the
shed, Riglett shambling behind at an interval of two yards.

Mr. Downing unlocked the door, and there on the floor
was the Clue!

A clue that even Doctor Watson could not have over-
looked.

Mr. Downing saw it, but did not immediately recognize
it for what it was.   What he saw at first was not a Clue,
but just a mess.   He had a tidy soul and abhorred messes.
And this was a particularly messy mess.   The greater part
of the flooring in the neighbourhood of the door was a sea of
red paint.   The tin from which it had flowed was lying on
its side in the middle of the shed.   The air was full of the
pungent scent.

"Pah!" said Mr. Downing.

Then suddenly, beneath the disguise of the mess, he saw
the clue.   A footmark!   No less.   A crimson footmark
on the grey concrete!

Riglett, who had been waiting patiently two yards away,
now coughed plaintively.   The sound recalled Mr. Downing to mundane matters.

"Get your bicycle, Riglett," he said, "and be careful
where you tread.   Somebody has upset a pot of paint on
the floor."

Riglett, walking delicately through dry places, extracted his bicycle from the rack, and presently departed to gladden the heart of his aunt, leaving Mr. Downing, his brain fizzing with the enthusiasm of the detective, to lock the door and resume his perambulation of the cricket field.

Give Doctor Watson a fair start, and he is a demon at the game. Mr. Downing's brain was now working with a rapidity and clearness which a professional sleuth might have envied.

Paint. Red paint. Obviously the same paint with which Sammy had been decorated. A footmark. Whose footmark? Plainly that of the criminal who had done the deed of decoration.

Yoicks!

There were two things, however, to be considered. Your careful detective, must consider everything. In the first place, the paint might have been upset by the groundsman. It was the groundsman's paint. He had been giving a fresh coating to the woodwork in front of the pavilion scoring-box at the conclusion of yesterday's match. (A labour of love which was the direct outcome of the enthusiasm for work which Adair had instilled into him.) In that case the footmark might be his.

Note one: Interview the groundsman on this point.

In the second place Adair might have upset the tin and trodden in its contents when he went to get his bicycle in order to fetch the doctor for the suffering MacPhee. This was the more probable of the two contingencies, for it would have been dark in the shed when Adair went into it.

Note two: Interview Adair as to whether he found, on returning to the house, that there was paint on his shoes.

Things were moving.

He resolved to take Adair first. He could get the groundsman's address from him.

Passing by the trees under whose shade Mike and Psmith and Dunster had watched the match on the previous day, he came upon the Head of his house in a deck-chair reading a book. A summer Sunday afternoon is the time for reading in deck-chairs.

"Oh, Adair," he said. "No, don't get up. I merely wished to ask you if you found any paint on your shoes when you returned to the house last night?"

"Paint, sir?" Adair was plainly puzzled. His book had been interesting, and had driven the Sammy incident out of his head.

"I see somebody has spilt some paint on the floor of the bicycle shed. You did not do that, I suppose, when you went to fetch your bicycle?"

"No, sir."

"It is spilt all over the floor. I wondered whether you had happened to tread in it. But you say you found no paint on your shoes this morning?"

"No, sir, my bicycle is always quite near the door of the shed. I didn't go into the shed at all."

"I see. Quite so. Thank you, Adair. Oh, by the way, Adair, where does Markby live?"

"I forget the name of his cottage, sir, but I could show you in a second. It's one of those cottages just past the school gates, on the right as you turn out into the road. There are three in a row. His is the first you come to. There's a barn just before you get to them."

"Thank you. I shall be able to find them. I should like to speak to Markby for a moment on a small matter."

A sharp walk took him to the cottages Adair had mentioned. He rapped at the door of the first, and the groundsman came out in his shirt-sleeves, blinking as if he had just woke up, as was indeed the case.

"Oh, Markby!"

"Sir?"

"You remember that you were painting the scoring-box in the pavilion last night after the match?"

"Yes, sir. It wanted a lick of paint bad. The young gentlemen will scramble about and get through the window. Makes it look shabby, sir. So I thought I'd better give it a coating so as to look shipshape when the Marylebone come down."

"Just so. An excellent idea. Tell me, Markby, what did you do with the pot of paint when you had finished?"

"Put it in the bicycle shed, sir."

"On the floor?"

"On the floor, sir? No. On the shelf at the far end, with the can of whitening what I use for marking out the wickets, sir."

"Of course, yes. Quite so. Just as I thought."

"Do you want it, sir?"

"No, thank you, Markby, no, thank you. The fact is, somebody who had no business to do so has moved the pot of paint from the shelf to the floor, with the result that it has been kicked over and spilt. You had better get some more tomorrow. Thank you, Markby. That is all I wished to know."

Mr. Downing walked back to the school thoroughly excited. He was hot on the scent now. The only other possible theories had been tested and successfully exploded. The thing had become simple to a degree. All he had to do was to go to Mr. Outwood's house—the idea of searching a fellow-master's house did not appear to him at all a delicate task; somehow one grew unconsciously to feel that Mr. Outwood did not really exist as a man capable of resenting liberties—find the paint-splashed shoe, ascertain its owner, and denounce him to the headmaster. There could be no doubt that a paint-splashed shoe must be in Mr. Outwood's house somewhere. A boy cannot tread in a pool of paint without showing some signs of having done so. It was Sunday, too, so that the shoe would not yet have been cleaned. Yoicks! Also Tally-ho! This really was beginning to be something like business.

Regardless of the heat, the sleuth-hound hurried across to Outwood's as fast as he could walk.

CHAPTER XX

A CHECK

THE only two members of the house not out in the grounds when he arrived were Mike and Psmith. They were standing on the gravel drive in front of the boys' entrance. Mike had a deck-chair in one hand and a book in the other. Psmith—for even the greatest minds will sometimes unbend—was wrestling with a yo-yo. That is to say, he was trying without success to keep the spool spinning. He smoothed a crease out of his waistcoat and tried again. He had just succeeded in getting the thing to spin when Mr. Downing arrived. The sound of his footsteps disturbed Psmith and brought the effort to nothing.

"Enough of this spoolery," said he, flinging the spool through the open window of the senior day-room. "I was an ass ever to try it. The philosophical minds needs complete repose in its hours of leisure. Hullo!"

He stared after the sleuth-hound, who had just entered the house.

"What the dickens," said Mike, "does he mean by barging in as if he'd bought the place?"

"Comrade Downing looks pleased with himself. What brings him round in this direction, I wonder! Still, no matter. The few articles which he may sneak from our study are of inconsiderable value. He is welcome to them. Do you feel inclined to wait awhile till I have fetched a chair and book?"

"I'll be going on. I shall be under the trees at the far end of the ground."

"'Tis well. I will be with you in about two ticks."

Mike walked on towards the field, and Psmith, strolling upstairs to fetch his novel, found Mr. Downing standing in the passage with the air of one who has lost his bearings.

"A warm afternoon, sir," murmured Psmith courteously, as he passed.

"Er—Smith!"

"Sir?"

"I—er—wish to go round the dormitories."

It was Psmith's guiding rule in life never to be surprised at anything, so he merely inclined his head gracefully, and said nothing.

"I should be glad if you would fetch the keys and show me where the rooms are."

"With acute pleasure, sir," said Psmith. "Or shall I fetch Mr. Outwood, sir?"

"Do as I tell you, Smith," snapped Mr. Downing.

Psmith said no more, but went down to the matron's room. The matron being out, he abstracted the bunch of keys from her table and rejoined the master.

"Shall I lead the way, sir?" he asked.

Mr. Downing nodded.

"Here, sir," said Psmith, opening a door, "we have Barnes's dormitory. An airy room, constructed on the soundest hygienic principles. Each boy, I understand, has quite a considerable number of cubic feet of air all to himself. It is Mr. Outwood's boast that no boy has ever asked for a cubic foot of air in vain. He argues justly——"

He broke off abruptly and began to watch the other's manœuvres in silence. Mr. Downing was peering rapidly beneath each bed in turn

"Are you looking for Barnes, sir?" inquired Psmith politely. "I think he's out in the field."

Mr. Downing rose, having examined the last bed, crimson in the face with the exercise.

"Show me the next dormitory, Smith," he said, panting slightly.

"This," said Psmith, opening the next door and sinking his voice to an awed whisper, "is where *I* sleep!"

Mr. Downing glanced swiftly beneath the three beds.

"Excuse me, sir," said Psmith, "but are we chasing anything?"

"Be good enough, Smith," said Mr. Downing with asperity, "to keep your remarks to yourself."

"I was only wondering, sir. Shall I show you the next in order?"

"Certainly."

They moved on up the passage.

Drawing blank at the last dormitory, Mr. Downing paused, baffled. Psmith waited patiently by. An idea struck the master.

"The studies, Smith," he cried.

"Aha!" said Psmith. "I beg your pardon, sir. The observation escaped me unawares. The frenzy of the chase is beginning to enter into my blood. Here we have——"

Mr. Downing stopped short.

"Is this impertinence studied, Smith?"

"Ferguson's study, sir? No, sir. That's farther down the passage. This is Barnes's."

Mr. Downing looked at him closely. Psmith's face was wooden in its gravity. The master snorted suspiciously, then moved on.

"Whose is this?" he asked, rapping a door.

"This, sir, is mine and Jackson's."

"What! Have you a study? You are low down in the school for it."

"I think, sir, that Mr. Outwood gave it us rather as a testimonial to our general worth than to our proficiency in school-work."

Mr. Downing raked the room with a keen eye. The absence of bars from the window attracted his attention.

"Have you no bars to your windows here, such as there are in my house?"

"There appears to be no bar, sir," said Psmith putting up his eyeglass.

Mr. Downing was leaning out of the window.

"A lovely view, is it not, sir?" said Psmith. "The trees, the field, the distant hills——"

Mr. Downing suddenly started. His eye had been caught by the water-pipe at the side of the window. The boy whom Sergeant Collard had seen climbing the pipe must have been making for this study.

He spun round and met Psmith's blandly inquiring gaze. He looked at Psmith carefully for a moment. No. The boy he had chased last night had not been Psmith. That exquisite's figure and general appearance were unmistakable, even in the dusk.

"Whom did you say you shared this study with, Smith?"

"Jackson, sir. The cricketer."

"Never mind about his cricket, Smith," said Mr. Downing with irritation.

"No, sir."

"He is the only other occupant of the room?"

"Yes, sir."

"Nobody else comes into it?"

"If they do, they go out extremely quickly, sir."

"Ah! Thank you, Smith."

"Not at all, sir."

Mr. Downing pondered. Jackson! The boy bore him a grudge. The boy was precisely the sort of boy to revenge himself by painting the dog Sammy. And, gadzooks! The boy whom he had pursued last night had been just about Jackson's size and build!

Mr. Downing was as firmly convinced at that moment that Mike's had been the hand to wield the paint-brush as he had ever been of anything in his life.

"Smith!" he said excitedly.

"On the spot, sir," said Psmith affably.

"Where are Jackson's shoes?"

There are moments when the giddy excitement of being right on the trail causes the amateur (or Watsonian) detective to be incautious. Such a moment came to Mr. Downing then. If he had been wise, he would have achieved his object, the getting a glimpse of Mike's shoes, by a devious and snaky route. As it was, he rushed straight on.

"His shoes, sir? He has them on. I noticed them as he went out just now."

"Where is the pair he wore yesterday?"

"Where are the shoes of yester-year?" murmured Psmith to himself. "I should say at a venture, sir, that they would be in the basket downstairs. Edmund, our genial knife-and-boot boy, collects them, I believe, at early dawn."

"Would they have been cleaned yet?"

"If I know Edmund, sir—no."

"Smith," said Mr. Downing, trembling with excitement, "go and bring that basket to me here."

Psmith's brain was working rapidly as he went downstairs. What exactly was at the back of the sleuth's mind, prompting these manœuvres, he did not know. But that there was something, and that that something was directed in a hostile manner against Mike, probably in connection with last night's wild happenings, he was certain. Psmith had noticed, on leaving his bed at the sound of the alarm bell, that he and Jellicoe were alone in the room. That might mean that Mike had gone out through the door when the bell sounded, or it might mean that he had been out all the time. It began to look as if the latter solution were the correct one.

He staggered back with the basket, painfully conscious all the while that it was creasing his waistcoat, and dumped it down on the study floor. Mr. Downing stooped eagerly over it. Psmith leaned against the wall, and straightened out the damaged garment.

"We have here, sir," he said, "a fair selection of our various bootings."

Mr. Downing looked up.

"You dropped none of the shoes on your way up, Smith?"

"Not one, sir. It was a fine performance."

Mr. Downing uttered a grunt of satisfaction, and bent once more to his task. Shoes flew about the room. Mr. Downing knelt on the floor beside the basket, and dug like a terrier at a rat-hole.

At last he made a dive, and, with an exclamation of triumph, rose to his feet. In his hand he held a shoe.

"Put those back again, Smith," he said.

The ex-Etonian, wearing an expression such as a martyr might have worn on being told off for the stake, began to pick up the scattered footgear, whistling softly the tune of "I do all the dirty work," as he did so.

"That's the lot, sir," he said, rising.

"Ah, Now come across with me to the headmaster's house. Leave the basket here. You can carry it back when you return."

"Shall I put back that shoe, sir?"

"Certainly not. I shall take this with me, of course."

"Shall I carry it, sir?"

Mr. Downing reflected.

"Yes, Smith," he said. "I think it would be best."

It occurred to him that the spectacle of a house-master wandering abroad on the public highway, carrying a dirty shoe, might be a trifle undignified. You never knew whom you might meet on Sunday afternoon.

Psmith took the shoe, and doing so, understood what before had puzzled him.

Across the toe of the shoe was a broad splash of red paint.

He knew nothing, of course, of the upset tin in the bicycle shed; but when a house-master's dog has been painted red in the night, and when, on the following day, the house-master goes about in search of a paint-splashed shoe, one puts two and two together. Psmith looked at the name inside the shoe. It was "Brown, bootmaker, Bridgnorth." Bridgnorth was only a few miles from his own home and Mike's. Undoubtedly it was Mike's shoe.

"Can you tell me whose shoe that is?" asked Mr. Downing.

Psmith looked at it again.

"No, sir. I can't say the little chap's familiar to me."

"Come with me, then."

Mr. Downing left the room. After a moment Psmith followed him.

The headmaster was in his garden. Thither Mr. Downing made his way, the shoe-bearing Psmith in close attendance.

The Head listened to the amateur detective's statement with interest.

"Indeed?" he said, when Mr. Downing had finished. "Indeed? Dear me! It certainly seems— It is a curiously well-connected thread of evidence. You are certain that there was red paint on this shoe you discovered in Mr. Outwood's house?"

"I have it with me. I brought it on purpose to show to you. Smith!"

"Sir?"

"You have the shoe?"

"Ah," said the headmaster, putting on a pair of pincenez, "now let me look at— This, you say, is the—? Just so. Just so. Just . . . But, er, Mr. Downing, it may be that I have not examined this shoe with sufficient care, but— Can *you* point out to me exactly where this paint is that you speak of?"

Mr. Downing stood staring at the shoe with a wild, fixed stare. Of any suspicion of paint, red or otherwise, it was absolutely and entirely innocent.

CHAPTER XXI

THE DESTROYER OF EVIDENCE

THE shoe became the centre of attraction, the cynosure of all eyes. Mr. Downing fixed it with the piercing stare of one who feels that his brain is tottering. The headmaster looked at it with a mildly puzzled expression. Psmith, putting up his eyeglass, gazed at it with a sort of affectionate interest, as if he were waiting for it to do a trick of some kind.

Mr. Downing was the first to break the silence.

"There was paint on this shoe," he said vehemently. "I tell you there was a splash of red paint across the toe. Smith will bear me out in this. Smith, you saw the paint on this shoe?"

"Paint, sir!"

"What! Do you mean to tell me that you did *not* see it?"

"No, sir. There was no paint on this shoe."

"This is foolery. I saw it with my own eyes. It was a broad splash right across the toe."

The headmaster interposed.

"You must have made a mistake, Mr. Downing. There is certainly no trace of paint on this shoe. These momentary optical delusions are, I fancy, not uncommon. Any doctor will tell you——"

"I had an aunt, sir," said Psmith chattily, "who was remarkably subject——"

"It is absurd. I cannot have been mistaken," said Mr. Downing. "I am positively certain the toe of this shoe was red when I found it."

"It is undoubtedly black now, Mr. Downing."

"A sort of chameleon shoe," murmured Psmith.

The goaded house-master turned on him.

"What did you say, Smith?"

"Did I speak, sir?" said Psmith, with the start of one coming suddenly out of a trance.

Mr. Downing looked searchingly at him.

"You had better be careful, Smith."

"Yes, sir."

"I strongly suspect you of having something to do with this."

"Really, Mr. Downing," said the headmaster, "that is surely improbable. Smith could scarcely have cleaned the shoe on his way to my house. On one occasion I inadvertently spilt some paint on a shoe of my own. I can assure you that it does not brush off. It needs a very systematic cleaning before all traces are removed."

"Exactly, sir," said Psmith. "My theory, if I may——?"

"Certainly Smith."

Psmith bowed courteously and proceeded.

"My theory, sir, is that Mr. Downing was deceived by the light and shade effects on the toe of the shoe. The afternoon sun, streaming in through the window, must have shone on the shoe in such a manner as to give it a momentary and fictitious aspect of redness. If Mr. Downing recollects, he did not look long at the shoe. The picture on the retina of the eye, consequently, had not time to fade. I remember thinking myself, at the moment, that the shoe appeared to have a certain reddish tint. The mistake——"

"Bah!" said Mr. Downing shortly.

"Well, really," said the headmaster, "it seems to me that that is the only explanation that will square with the facts. A shoe that is really smeared with red paint does not become black of itself in the course of a few minutes."

"You are very right, sir," said Psmith with benevolent approval. "May I go now, sir? I am in the middle of a singularly impressive passage of Cicero's speech De Senectute."

"I am sorry that you should leave your preparation till Sunday, Smith. It is a habit of which I altogether disapprove."

"I am reading it, sir," said Psmith, with simple dignity, "for pleasure. Shall I take the shoe with me, sir?"

"If Mr. Downing does not want it?"

The house-master passed the fraudulent piece of evidence to Psmith without a word, and the latter, having included both masters in a kindly smile, left the garden.

Pedestrians who had the good fortune to be passing along the road between the headmaster's house and Mr. Outwood's at that moment saw what, if they had but known it, was a most unusual sight, the spectacle of Psmith running. Psmith's usual mode of progression was a dignified walk. He believed in the contemplative style rather than the hustling.

On this occasion, however, reckless of possible injuries to the crease of his trousers, he raced down the road, and turning in at Outwood's gate, bounded upstairs like a highly trained professional athlete.

On arriving at the study, his first act was to remove a shoe from the top of the pile in the basket, place it in the small cupboard under the bookshelf, and lock the cupboard. Then he flung himself into a chair and panted.

"Brain," he said to himself approvingly, "is what one chiefly needs in matters of this kind. Without brain, where are we? In the soup, every time. The next development will be when Comrade Downing thinks it over, and is struck with the brilliant idea that it's just possible that the shoe he gave me to carry and the shoe I did carry were not one shoe but two shoes. Meanwhile——"

He dragged up another chair for his feet and picked up his novel.

He had not been reading long when there was a footstep in the passage, and Mr. Downing appeared.

The possibility, in fact the probability, of Psmith having substituted another shoe for the one with the incriminating splash of paint on it had occurred to him almost immediately on leaving the headmaster's garden. Psmith and Mike, he reflected, were friends. Psmith's impulse would be to do all that lay in his power to shield Mike. Feeling aggrieved with himself that he had not thought of this before, he, too, hurried over to Outwood's.

Mr. Downing was brisk and peremptory.

"I wish to look at these shoes again," he said. Psmith, with a sigh, laid down his novel, and rose to assist him.

"Sit down, Smith," said the house-master. "I can manage without your help."

Psmith sat down again, carefully tucking up the knees of his trousers, and watched him with silent interest through his eyeglass.

The scrutiny irritated Mr. Downing.

"Put that thing away, Smith," he said.

"That thing, sir?"

"Yes, that ridiculous glass. Put it away."

"Why, sir?"

"Why! Because I tell you to do so."

"I guessed that that was the reason, sir," sighed Psmith, replacing the eyeglass in his waistcoat pocket. He rested his elbows on his knees, and his chin on his hands, and resumed his contemplative inspection of the shoe-expert, who, after fidgeting for a few moments, lodged another complaint.

"Don't sit there staring at me, Smith."

"I was interested in what you were doing, sir."

"Never mind. Don't stare at me in that idiotic way."

"May I read, sir?" asked Psmith, patiently.

"Yes, read if you like."

"Thank you, sir."

Psmith took up his book again, and Mr. Downing, now thoroughly irritated, pursued his investigations in the boot-basket.

He went through it twice, but each time without success. After the second search, he stood up, and looked wildly round the room. He was as certain as he could be of anything that the missing piece of evidence was somewhere in the study. It was no use asking Psmith point-blank where it was, for Psmith's ability to parry dangerous questions with evasive answers was quite out of the common.

His eye roamed about the room. There was very little cover there, even for so small a fugitive as a number nine shoe. The floor could be acquitted, on sight, of harbouring the quarry.

Then he caught sight of the cupboard, and something seemed to tell him that there was the place to look.

"Smith!" he said.

Psmith had been reading placidly all the while.

"Yes, sir?"

"What is in this cupboard?"

"That cupboard, sir?"

"Yes. This cupboard." Mr. Downing rapped the door irritably.

"Just a few odd trifles, sir. We do not often use it. A ball of string, perhaps. Possibly an old notebook. Nothing of value or interest.

"Open it."

"I think you will find that it is locked, sir."

"Unlock it."

"But where is the key, sir?"

"Have you not got the key?"

"If the key is not in the lock, sir, you may depend upon it that it will take a long search to find it."

"Where did you see it last?"

"It was in the lock yesterday morning   Jackson might have taken it."

"Where is Jackson?"

"Out in the field somewhere, sir."

Mr. Downing thought for a moment.

"I don't believe a word of it," he said shortly. "I have my reasons for thinking that you are deliberately keeping the contents of that cupboard from me. I shall break open the door."

Psmith got up.

"I'm afraid you mustn't do that, sir."

Mr. Downing stared, amazed.

"Are you aware whom you are talking to Smith?" he inquired icily.

"Yes, sir. And I know it's not Mr. Outwood, to whom that cupboard happens to belong. If you wish to break it open, you must get his permission. He is the sole lessee and proprietor of that cupboard. I am only the acting manager."

Mr. Downing paused. He also reflected. Mr. Outwood in the general rule did not count much in the scheme of things, but possibly there were limits to the treating of him as if he did not exist. To enter his house without his permission and search it to a certain extent was all very well. But when it came to breaking up his furniture, perhaps——!

On the other hand, there was the maddening thought that if he left the study in search of Mr. Outwood, in order to obtain his sanction for the house-breaking work which he proposed to carry through, Smith would be alone in the room. And he knew that if Smith were left alone in the room, he would instantly remove the shoe to some other hiding-place. He thoroughly disbelieved the story of the lost key. He was perfectly convinced that the missing shoe was in the cupboard.

He stood chewing these thoughts for a while, Psmith in the meantime standing in a graceful attitude in front of the cupboard, staring into vacancy.

Then he was seized with a happy idea. Why should he leave the room at all? If he sent Smith, then he himself could wait and make certain that the cupboard was not tampered with.

"Smith," he said, "go and find Mr. Outwood, and ask him to be good enough to come here for a moment."

CHAPTER XXII

MAINLY ABOUT SHOES

"Be quick, Smith," he said, as the latter stood looking at him without making any movement in the direction of the door."

"*Quick*, sir?" said Psmith meditatively, as if he had been asked a conundrum.

"Go and find Mr. Outwood at once."

Psmith still made no move.

"Do you intend to disobey me, Smith?" Mr. Downing's voice was steely.

"Yes, sir."

"What!"

"Yes, sir."

There was one of those you-could-have-heard-a-pin-drop silences. Psmith was staring reflectively at the ceiling. Mr. Downing was looking as if at any moment he might say, "Thwarted to me face, ha, ha! And by a very stripling!"

It was Psmith, however, who resumed the conversation. His manner was almost too respectful; which made it all the more a pity that what he said did not keep up the standard of docility.

"I take my stand," he said, "on a technical point. I say to myself, 'Mr. Downing is a man I admire as a human being and respect as a master. In——'"

"This impertinence is doing you no good, Smith."

Psmith waved a hand deprecatingly.

"If you will let me explain, sir. I was about to say that in any other place but Mr. Outwood's house, your word would be law. I would fly to do your bidding. If you pressed a button, I would do the rest. But in Mr. Outwood's house I cannot do anything except what pleases me or what is ordered by Mr. Outwood. I ought to have remembered that before. One cannot," he continued, as who should say, "Let us be reasonable," "one cannot, to take a parallel case, imagine the colonel commanding the garrison at a naval station going on board a battleship and ordering the crew to splice the jibboom spanker. It might be an admirable thing for the Empire that the jibboom spanker *should* be spliced at that particular juncture, but the crew would naturally decline to move in the matter until the order came from the commander of the ship. So in my case. If you will go to Mr. Outwood, and explain to him how matters stand, and come back and say to me, 'Psmith, Mr. Outwood wishes you to ask him to be good enough to come to this study,' then I shall be only too glad to go and find him. You see my difficulty, sir?"

"Go and fetch Mr. Outwood, Smith. I shall not tell you again."

Psmith flicked a speck of dust from his coat-sleeve.

"Very well, Smith."

"I can assure you, sir, at any rate, that if there is a shoe in that cupboard now, there will be a shoe there when you return."

Mr. Downing stalked out of the room.

"But," added Psmith pensively to himself, as the footsteps died away, "I did not promise that it would be the same shoe."

He took the key from his pocket, unlocked the cupboard, and took out the shoe. Then he selected from the basket a particularly battered specimen. Placing this in the cupboard, he re-locked the door.

His next act was to take from the shelf a piece of string. Attaching one end of this to the shoe that he had taken from the cupboard, he went to the window. His first act was to fling the cupboard-key out into the bushes. Then he turned to the shoe. On a level with the sill the water-pipe, up which Mike had started to climb the night before, was fastened to the wall by an iron band. He tied the other end of the string to this, and let the shoe swing free. He noticed with approval, when it had stopped swinging, that it was hidden from above by the window-sill.

He returned to his place at the mantelpiece.

As an afterthought he took another shoe from the basket, and thrust it up the chimney. A shower of soot fell into the grate, blackening his hand.

The bathroom was a few yards down the corridor. He went there, and washed off the soot.

When he returned, Mr. Downing was in the study, and with him Mr. Outwood, the latter looking dazed, as if he were not quite equal to the intellectual pressure of the situation.

"Where have you been, Smith?" asked Mr. Downing sharply.

"I have been washing my hands, sir."

"H'm!" said Mr. Downing suspiciously.

"Yes, I saw Smith go into the bathroom," said Mr. Outwood. "Smith, I cannot quite understand what it is Mr. Downing wishes me to do."

"My dear Outwood," snapped the sleuth, "I thought I had made it perfectly clear. Where is the difficulty?"

"I cannot understand why you should suspect Smith of keeping his shoes in a cupboard, and," added Mr. Outwood with spirit, catching sight of a Good-Gracious-has-the-man-*no*-sense look on the other's face, "why he should not do so if he wishes it."

"Exactly, sir," said Psmith, approvingly. "You have touched the spot."

"If I must explain again, my dear Outwood, will you kindly give me your attention for a moment. Last night a boy broke out of your house, and painted my dog Sampson red."

"He painted——!" said Mr. Outwood, round-eyed. "Why?"

"I don't know why. At any rate, he did. During the escapade one of his shoes was splashed with the paint. It is that shoe which I believe Smith to be concealing in this cupboard. Now, do you understand?"

Mr. Outwood looked amazedly at Smith, and Psmith shook his head sorrowfully at Mr. Outwood. Psmith's expression said, as plainly as if he had spoken the words, "We must humour him."

"So with your permission, as Smith declares that he has lost the key, I propose to break open the door of this cupboard. Have you any objection?"

Mr. Outwood started.

"Objection? None at all, my dear fellow, none at all. Let me see, *what* is it you wish to do?"

"This," said Mr. Downing shortly.

There was a pair of dumb-bells on the floor, belonging to Mike. He never used them, but they always managed to get themselves packed with the rest of his belongings on the last day of the holidays. Mr. Downing seized one of these, and delivered two rapid blows at the cupboard-door. The wood splintered. A third blow smashed the flimsy lock. The cupboard, with any skeletons it might contain, was open for all to view.

Mr. Downing uttered a cry of triumph, and tore the shoe from its resting-place.

"I told you," he said. "I told you."

"I wondered where that shoe had got to," said Psmith. "I've been looking for it for days."

Mr. Downing was examining his find. He looked up with an exclamation of surprise and wrath.

"This shoe has no paint on it," he said, glaring at Psmith. "This is not the shoe."

"It certainly appears, sir," said Psmith sympathetically, "to be free from paint. There's a sort of reddish glow just there, if you look at it sideways," he added helpfully.

"Did you place that shoe there, Smith?"

"I must have done. Then, when I lost the key——"

"Are you satisfied now, Downing?" interrupted Mr. Outwood with asperity, "or is there any more furniture you wish to break?"

The excitement of seeing his household goods smashed with a dumb-bell had made the archæological student quite a swashbuckler for the moment. A little more, and one could imagine him giving Mr. Downing a good, hard knock.

The sleuth-hound stood still for a moment, baffled. But his brain was working with the rapidity of a buzz-saw. A chance remark of Mr. Outwood's set him fizzing off on the trail once more. Mr. Outwood had caught sight of the little pile of soot in the grate. He bent down to inspect it.

"Dear me," he said, "I must remember to have the chimneys swept. It should have been done before."

Mr. Downing's eye, rolling in a fine frenzy from heaven to earth, from earth to heaven, also focused itself on the pile of soot; and a thrill went through him. Soot in the fireplace! Smith washing his hands! ("You know my methods, my dear Watson. Apply them.")

Mr. Downing's mind at that moment contained one single thought; and that thought was "What ho for the chimney!"

He dived forward with a rush, nearly knocking Mr. Outwood off his feet, and thrust an arm up into the unknown. An avalanche of soot fell upon his hand and wrist, but he ignored it, for at the same instant his fingers had closed upon what he was seeking.

"Ah," he said. "I thought as much. You were not quite clever enough, after all, Smith."

"No, sir," said Psmith patiently. "We all make mistakes."

"You would have done better, Smith, not to have given me all this trouble. You have done yourself no good by it."

"It's been great fun, though, sir," argued Psmith.

"Fun!" Mr. Downing laughed grimly. "You may have reason to change your opinion of what constitutes——"

His voice failed as his eye fell on the all-black toe of the shoe. He looked up, and caught Psmith's benevolent gaze. He straightened himself and brushed a bead of perspiration from his face with the back of his hand.   Unfortunately, he used the sooty hand, and the result was like some gruesome burlesque of a nigger minstrel.

"Did - you - put - that - shoe - there, Smith?" he asked slowly.

"Yes, sir."

"Then what did you *MEAN* by putting it there?" roared Mr. Downing.

"Animal spirits, sir," said Psmith.

"WHAT?"

"Animal spirits, sir."

What Mr. Downing would have replied to this one cannot tell, though one can guess roughly.   For, just as he was opening his mouth, Mr. Outwood, catching sight of his nigger-like countenance, intervened.

"My dear Downing," he said, "your face. It is positively covered with soot, positively. You must come and wash it. You are quite black. Really you present a most curious appearance, most. Let me show you the way to my room."

In all times of storm and tribulation there comes a breaking-point, a point where the spirit definitely refuses to battle any longer against the slings and arrows of outrageous fortune.   Mr. Downing could not bear up against this crowning blow.   He went down beneath it.   In the language of the Ring, he took the count.   It was the knock-out.

"Soot!" he murmured weakly.   "Soot!"

"Your face is covered, my dear fellow, quite covered."

"It certainly has a faintly sooty aspect, sir," said Psmith.

His voice roused the sufferer to one last flicker of spirit.

"You will hear more of this, Smith," he said.   "I say you will hear more of it."

Then he allowed Mr. Outwood to lead him out to a place where there were towels, soap, and sponges.

When they had gone, Psmith went to the window, and hauled in the string.   He felt the calm afterglow which comes to the general after a successfully conducted battle. It had been trying, of course, for a man of refinement, and it had cut into his afternoon, but on the whole it had been worth it.

The problem now was what to do with the painted shoe. It would take a lot of cleaning, he saw, even if he could get hold of the necessary implements for cleaning it. And he rather doubted if he would be able to do so. Edmund, the boot-boy, worked in some mysterious cell far from the madding crowd, at the back of the house. In the boot-cupboard downstairs there would probable be nothing likely to be of any use.

His fears were realized. The boot-cupboard was empty. It seemed to him that, for the time being, the best thing he could do would be to place the shoe in safe hiding, until he should have thought out a scheme.

Having restored the basket to its proper place, accordingly, he went up to the study again, and placed the red-toed shoe in the chimney, at about the same height where Mr. Downing had found the other. Nobody would think of looking there a second time, and it was improbable that Mr. Outwood really would have the chimneys swept, as he had said. The odds were that he had forgotten about it already.

Psmith went to the bathroom to wash his hands again, with the feeling that he had done a good day's work.

CHAPTER XXIII

ON THE TRAIL AGAIN

THE most massive minds are apt to forget things at times.
most adroit plotters make their little mistakes. Psmith
was no exception to the rule. He made the mistake of not
telling Mike of the afternoon's happenings.

It was not altogether forgetfulness. Psmith was one
of those people who like to carry through their operations
entirely by themselves. Where there is only one in a secret
the secret is more liable to remain unrevealed. There was
nothing, he thought, to be gained from telling Mike. He
forgot what the consequences might be if he did not.

So Psmith kept his own counsel, with the result that Mike
went over to school on the Monday morning in gym shoes.

Edmund, summoned from the hinterland of the house to
give his opinion why only one of Mike's shoes was to be
found, had no views on the subject. He seemed to look on
it as one of those things which no fellow can understand.

"'Ere's one of 'em, Mr. Jackson," he said, as if he hoped
that Mike might be satisfied with a compromise.

"One? What's the good of that, Edmund, you chump?
I can't go over to school in one shoe."

Edmund turned this over in his mind, and then said,
"No, sir," as much as to say, "I may have lost a shoe, but,
thank goodness, I can still understand sound reasoning."

"Well, what am I to do? Where *is* the other shoe?"

"Don't know, Mr. Jackson," replied Edmund to both
questions.

"Well, I mean—— Oh, dash it, there's the bell."
And Mike sprinted off in the gym shoes he stood in.

It is only a deviation from those ordinary rules of school

life, which one observes naturally and without thinking, that enables one to realize how strong public-school prejudices really are. At a school, for instance, where the regulations say that coats only of black or dark blue are to be worn, a boy who appears one day in even the most respectable and unostentatious brown finds himself looked on with a mixture of awe and repulsion, which would be excessive if he had sand-bagged the headmaster. So in the case of shoes. School rules decree that a boy shall go to his form-room in shoes. There is no real reason why, if the day is fine, he should not wear gym shoes, should he prefer them. But, if he does, the thing creates a perfect sensation. Boys say, "Great Scot, what *have* you got on?" Masters say, "Jones, *what* are you wearing on your feet?" In the few minutes which elapse between the assembling of the form for call-over and the arrival of the form-master, some wag is sure either to stamp on the gym shoes, accompanying the act with some satirical remark, or else to pull one of them off, and inaugurate an impromptu game of football with it. There was once a boy who went to school one morning in elastic-sided boots.

Mike had always been coldly distant in his relations to the rest of his form, looking on them, with a few exceptions, as worms; and the form, since his innings against Downing's on the Friday, had regarded Mike with respect. So that he escaped the ragging he would have had to undergo at Wrykyn in similar circumstances. It was only Mr. Downing who gave trouble.

There is a sort of instinct which enables some masters to tell when a boy in their form is wearing gym shoes instead of the more formal kind, just as people who dislike cats always know when one is in a room with them. They cannot see it but they feel it in their bones.

Mr. Downing was perhaps the most bigoted anti-gym-shoeist in the whole list of English schoolmasters. He waged war remorselessly against gym shoes. Satire, abuse, lines, detention—every weapon was employed by him in dealing with their wearers. It had been the late Dunster's

142

practice always to go over to school in gym shoes when, as he usually did, he felt shaky in the morning's lesson. Mr. Downing always detected him in the first five minutes, and that meant a lecture of anything from ten minutes to a quarter of an hour on Untidy Habits and Boys Who Looked like Loafers—which broke the back of the morning's work nicely. On one occasion, when a particularly tricky bit of Livy was on the bill of fare, Dunster had entered the form-room in heel-less Turkish bath-slippers, of a vivid crimson; and the subsequent proceedings, including his journey over to the house to change the heel-less atrocities, had seen him through very nearly to the quarter to eleven interval.

Mike, accordingly, had not been in his place for three minutes when Mr. Downing, stiffening like a pointer, called his name.

"Yes, sir?" said Mike.

"*What* are you wearing on your feet, Jackson?"

"Gym shoes, sir."

"You are wearing gym shoes? Are you not aware that gym shoes are not the proper things to come to school in? Why are you wearing gym shoes?"

The form, leaning back against the next row of desks, settled itself comfortably for the address from the throne.

"I have lost one of my shoes, sir."

A kind of gulp escaped from Mr. Downing's lips. He stared at Mike for a moment in silence. Then, turning to Stone, he told him to start translating.

Stone, who had been expecting at least ten minutes' respite, was taken unawares. When he found the place in his book and began to construe, he floundered hopelessly. But, to his growing surprise and satisfaction, the form-master appeared to notice nothing wrong. He said "Yes, yes," mechanically, and finally, "That will do," where-upon Stone resumed his seat with the feeling that the age of miracles had returned.

Mr. Downing's mind was in a whirl. His case was

complete. Mike's appearance in gym shoes, with the explanation that he had lost a shoe, completed the chain. As Columbus must have felt when his ship ran into harbour, and the first American interviewer, jumping on board, said, "Wal, sir, and what are your impressions of our glorious country?" so did Mr. Downing feel at that moment.

When the bell rang at a quarter to eleven, he gathered up his gown, and sped to the headmaster.

CHAPTER XXIV

THE ADAIR METHOD

IT was during the interval that day that Stone and Robinson, discussing the subject of cricket over a bun and ginger-beer at the school shop, came to a momentous decision, to wit, that they were fed up with the Adair administration and meant to strike. The immediate cause of revolt was early-morning fielding-practice, that searching test of cricket keenness. Mike himself, to whom cricket was the great and serious interest in life, had shirked early-morning fielding-practice in his first term at Wrykyn. And Stone and Robinson had but a lukewarm attachment to the game, compared with Mike's.

As a rule, Adair had contented himself with practice in the afternoon after school, which nobody objects to; and no strain, consequently, had been put upon Stone's and Robinson's allegiance. In view of the M.C.C. match on the Wednesday, however, he had now added to this an extra dose to be taken before breakfast. Stone and Robinson had left their comfortable beds that day at six o'clock, yawning and heavy-eyed, and had caught catches and fielded drives which, in the cool morning air, had stung like adders and bitten like serpents. Until the sun has really got to work, it is no joke taking a high catch. Stone's dislike of the experiment was only equalled by Robinson's. They were neither of them of the type which likes to undergo hardships for the common good. They played well enough when on the field, but neither cared greatly whether the school had a good season or not. They played the games entirely for their own sakes.

The result was that they went back to the house for breakfast with a never-again feeling, and at the earliest possible moment met to debate as to what was to be done about it. At all costs another experience like today's must be avoided.

"It's all rot," said Stone. "What on earth's the good of sweating about before breakfast? It only makes you tired."

"I shouldn't wonder," said Robinson, "if it wasn't bad for the heart. Rushing about on an empty stomach, I mean, and all that sort of thing."

"Personally," said Stone, gnawing his bun, "I don't intend to stick it."

"Nor do I."

"I mean, it's such absolute rot. If we aren't good enough to play for the team without having to get up overnight to catch catches, he'd better find somebody else."

"Yes."

At this moment Adair came into the shop.

"Fielding-practice again tomorrow," he said briskly, "at six."

"Before breakfast?" said Robinson.

"Rather. You two must buck up, you know. You were rotten today." And he passed on, leaving the two malcontents speechless.

Stone was the first to recover.

"I'm hanged if I turn out tomorrow," he said, as they left the shop. "He can do what he likes about it. Besides, what can he do, after all? Only kick us out of the team. And I don't mind that."

"Nor do I."

"I don't think he will kick us out, either. He can't play the M.C.C. with a scratch team. If he does, we'll go and play for that village Jackson plays for. We'll get Jackson to shove us into the team."

"All right," said Robinson. "Let's."

Their position was a strong one. A cricket captain may seem to be an autocrat of tremendous power, but in reality he has only one weapon, the keenness of those under him. With the majority, of course, the fear of being excluded or ejected from a team is a spur that drives. The majority, consequently, are easily handled. But when a cricket captain runs up against a boy who does not much care whether he plays for the team or not, then he finds himself in a difficult position, and, unless he is a man of action, practically helpless.

Stone and Robinson felt secure. Taking it all round, they felt that they would just as soon play for Lower Borlock as for the school. The bowling of the opposition would be weaker in the former case, and the chance of making runs greater. To a certain type of cricketer runs are runs, wherever and however made.

The result of all this was that Adair, turning out with the team next morning for fielding-practice, found himself two short. Barnes was among those present, but of the other two representatives of Outwood's house there were no signs.

Barnes, questioned on the subject, had no information to give, beyond the fact that he had not seen them about anywhere. Which was not a great help. Adair proceeded with the fielding-practice without further delay.

At breakfast that morning he was silent and apparently rapt in thought. Mr. Downing, who sat at the top of the table with Adair on his right, was accustomed at the morning meal to blend nourishment of the body with that of the mind. As a rule he had ten minutes with the daily paper before the bell rang, and it was his practice to hand on the results of his reading to Adair and the other house-prefects, who, not having seen the paper, usually formed an interested and appreciative audience. Today, however, though the house-prefects expressed varying degrees of excitement at the news that Sheppard had made a century against Gloucestershire, and that a butter famine was expected in the United States, these world-shaking news-items seemed to leave Adair cold. He champed his bread and marmalade with an abstracted air.

He was wondering what to do in the matter of Stone and Robinson.

Many captains might have passed the thing over. To take it for granted that the missing pair had overslept themselves would have been a safe and convenient way out of the difficulty. But Adair was not the sort of person who seeks for safe and convenient ways out of difficulties. He never shirked anything, physical or moral.

He resolved to interview the absentees.

It was not until after school that an opportunity offered itself. He went across to Outwood's and found the two non-starters in the senior day-room, engaged in the intellectual pursuit of kicking the wall and marking the height of each kick with chalk. Adair's entrance coincided with a record effort by Stone, which caused the kicker to overbalance and stagger backwards against the captain.

"Sorry," said Stone. "Hullo, Adair!"

"Don't mention it. Why weren't you two at fielding-practice this morning?"

Robinson, who left the lead to Stone in all matters, said nothing. Stone spoke.

"We didn't turn up," he said.

"I know you didn't. Why not?"

Stone had rehearsed this scene in his mind, and he spoke with the coolness which comes from rehearsal.

"We decided not to."

"Oh?"

"Yes. We came to the conclusion that we hadn't any use for early-morning fielding."

Adair's manner became ominously calm.

"You were rather fed-up, I suppose?"

"That's just the word."

"Sorry it bored you."

"It didn't. We didn't give it the chance to."

Robinson laughed appreciatively.

"What's the joke, Robinson?" asked Adair.

"There's no joke," said Robinson, with some haste. "I was only thinking of something."

"I'll give you something else to think about soon."

Stone intervened.

"It's no good making a row about it, Adair. You must see that you can't do anything. Of course, you can kick us out of the team, if you like, but we don't care if you do.

148

Jackson will get us a game any Wednesday or Saturday for the village he plays for. So we're all right. And the school team aren't such a lot of flyers that you can afford to go chucking people out of it whenever you want to. See what I mean?"

"You and Jackson seem to have fixed it all up between you."

"What are you going to do? Kick us out?"

"No."

"Good. I thought you'd see it was no good making a beastly row. We'll play for the school all right. There's no earthly need for us to turn out for fielding-practice before breakfast."

"You don't think there is? You may be right. All the same, you're going to tomorrow morning."

"What!"

"Six sharp. Don't be late."

"Don't be an ass, Adair. We've told you we aren't going to."

"That's only your opinion. I think you are. I'll give you till five past six, as you seem to like lying in bed."

"You can turn out if you feel like it. You won't find me there."

"That'll be a disappointment. Nor Robinson?"

"No," said the junior partner in the firm; but he said it without any deep conviction. The atmosphere was growing a great deal too tense for his comfort.

"You've quite made up your minds?"

"Yes," said Stone.

"Right," said Adair quietly, and knocked him down.

He was up again in a moment. Adair had pushed the table back, and was standing in the middle of the open space.

"You cad," said Stone. "I wasn't ready."

"Well, you are now. Shall we go on?"

Stone dashed in without a word, and for a few moments the two might have seemed evenly matched to a not too intelligent spectator. But science tells, even in a confined

149

space. Adair was smaller and lighter than Stone, but he was cooler and quicker, and he knew more about the game. His blow was always home a fraction of a second sooner than his opponent's. At the end of a minute Stone was on the floor again.

He got up slowly and stood leaning with one hand on the table.

"Suppose we say ten past six!" said Adair. "I'm not particular to a minute or two."

Stone made no reply.

"Will ten past six suit you for fielding-practice to-morrow?" said Adair.

"All right," said Stone.

"Thanks. How about you, Robinson?"

Robinson had been a petrified spectator of the Captain-Kettle-like manœuvres of the cricket captain, and it did not take him long to make up his mind. He was not altogether a coward. In different circumstances he might have put up a respectable show. But it takes a more than ordinarily courageous person to embark on a fight which he knows must end in his destruction. Robinson knew that he was nothing like a match even for Stone, and Adair had disposed of Stone in a little over one minute. It seemed to Robinson that neither pleasure nor profit was likely to come from an encounter with Adair.

"All right," he said hastily, "I'll turn up."

"Good," said Adair. "I wonder if either of you chaps could tell me which is Jackson's study."

Stone was dabbing at his mouth with a handkerchief, a task which precluded anything in the shape of conversation; so Robinson replied that Mike's study was the first you came to on the right of the corridor at the top of the stairs.

"Thanks," said Adair. "You don't happen to know if he's in, I suppose?"

"He went up with Smith a quarter of an hour ago. I don't know if he's still there."

"I'll go and see," said Adair. "I should like a word with him if he isn't busy."

CHAPTER XXV

ADAIR HAS A WORD WITH MIKE

MIKE, all unconscious of the stirring proceedings which had been going on below stairs, was peacefully reading a letter he had received that morning from Strachan at Wrykyn, in which the successor to the cricket captaincy which should have been Mike's had a good deal to say in a lugubrious strain. In Mike's absence things had been going badly with Wrykyn. A broken arm, contracted in the course of some rash experiments with a day-boy's motor-bicycle, had deprived the team of the services of Dunstable, the only man who had shown any signs of being able to bowl a side out. Since this calamity, wrote Strachan, everything had gone wrong. The M.C.C., led by Mike's brother Reggie, the least of the three first-class cricketing Jacksons, had smashed them by a hundred and fifty runs. Geddington had wiped them off the face of the earth. The Incogs, with a team recruited exclusively from the rabbit-hutch—not a well-known man on the side except Stacey, a veteran who had been playing for the club for nearly half a century—had got home by two wickets. In fact, it was Strachan's opinion that the Wrykyn team that summer was about the most hopeless gang of deadbeats that had ever made an exhibition of itself on the school grounds. The Ripton match, fortunately, was off, owing to an outbreak of mumps at that shrine of learning and athletics—the second outbreak of the malady in two terms. Which, said Strachan, was hard lines on Ripton, but a bit of jolly good luck for Wrykyn, as it had saved them from what would probably have been a record hammering, Ripton having eight of their last year's team left, including Dixon, the fast bowler, against whom Mike alone of the Wrykyn team had been able to make runs in the previous season Altogether, Wrykyn had struck a bad patch.

Mike mourned over his suffering school. If only he could have been there to help. It might have made all the difference. In school cricket one good batsman, to go in first and knock the bowlers off their length, may take a weak team triumphantly through a season. In school cricket the importance of a good start for the first wicket is incalculable.

As he put Strachan's letter away in his pocket, all his old bitterness against Sedleigh, which had been ebbing during the past few days, returned with a rush. He was conscious once more of that feeling of personal injury which had made him hate his new school on the first day of term.

And it was at this point, when his resentment was at its height, that Adair, the concrete representative of everything Sedleighan, entered the room.

There are moments in life's placid course when there has got to be the biggest kind of row. This was one of them.

Psmith, who was leaning against the mantelpiece, reading the serial story in a daily paper which he had abstracted from the senior day-room, made the intruder free of the study with a dignified wave of the hand, and went on reading. Mike remained in the deck-chair in which he was sitting, and contented himself with glaring at the newcomer.

Psmith was the first to speak.

"If you ask my candid opinion," he said, looking up from his paper, "I should say that young Lord Antony Trefusis was in the soup already. I seem to see the *consommé* splashing about his ankles. He's had a note telling him to be under the oak-tree in the Park at midnight. He's just off there at the end of this instalment. I bet Long Jack, the poacher, is waiting there with a sandbag. Care to see the paper, Comrade Adair? Or don't you take any interest in contemporary literature?"

"Thanks," said Adair. "I just wanted to speak to Jackson for a minute."

"Fate," said Psmith, "has led your footsteps to the right place. That is Comrade Jackson, the Pride of the School, sitting before you."

"What do you want?" said Mike.

He suspected that Adair had come to ask him once again to play for the school. The fact that the M.C.C. match was on the following day made this a probable solution of the reason for his visit. He could think of no other errand that was likely to have set the head of Downing's paying afternoon calls.

"I'll tell you in a minute. It won't take long."

"That," said Psmith approvingly, "is right. Speed is the key-note of the present age. Promptitude. Despatch. This is no time for loitering. We must be strenuous. We must hustle. We must Do It Now. We——"

"Buck up," said Mike.

"Certainly," said Adair. "I've just been talking to Stone and Robinson."

"An excellent way of passing an idle half-hour," said Psmith.

"We weren't exactly idle," said Adair grimly. "It didn't last long, but it was pretty lively while it did. Stone chucked it after the first round."

Mike got up out of his chair. He could not quite follow what all this was about, but there was no mistaking the truculence of Adair's manner. For some reason, which might possibly be made clear later, Adair was looking for trouble, and Mike in his present mood felt that it would be a privilege to see that he got it.

Psmith was regarding Adair through his eyeglass with pain and surprise.

"Surely," he said, "you do not mean us to understand that you have been *brawling* with Comrade Stone! This is bad hearing. I thought that you and he were like brothers. Such a bad example for Comrade Robinson, too. Leave us,

Adair. We would brood. Oh, go thee, knave, I'll none of thee. Shakespeare."

Psmith turned away, and resting his elbows on the mantel-piece, gazed at himself mournfully in the looking-glass.

"I'm not the man I was," he sighed, after a prolonged inspection. "There are lines on my face, dark circles beneath my eyes. The fierce rush of life at Sedleigh is wasting me away."

"Stone and I had a discussion about early-morning fielding-practice," said Adair, turning to Mike.

Mike said nothing.

"I thought his fielding wanted working up a bit, so I told him to turn out at six tomorrow morning. He said he wouldn't, so we argued it out. He's going to all right. So is Robinson."

Mike remained silent.

"So are you," said Adair.

"I get thinner and thinner," said Psmith from the mantel-piece.

Mike looked at Adair, and Adair looked at Mike, after the manner of two dogs before they fly at one another. There was an electric silence in the study. Psmith peered with increased earnestness into the glass.

"Oh?" said Mike at last. "What makes you think that?"

"I don't think. I know."

"Any special reason for my turning out?"

"Yes."

"What's that?"

"You're going to play for the school against the M.C.C. tomorrow, and I want you to get some practice."

"I wonder how you got that idea!"

"Curious I should have done, isn't it?"

"Very. You aren't building on it much, are you?" said Mike politely.

"I am, rather," replied Adair, with equal courtesy.

"I'm afraid you'll be disappointed."

"I don't think so."

"My eyes," said Psmith regretfully, "are a bit close together. However," he added philosophically, "it's too late to alter that now."

Mike drew a step closer to Adair.

"What makes you think I shall play against the M.C.C.?" he asked curiously.

"I'm going to make you."

Mike took another step forward. Adair moved to meet him.

"Would you care to try now?" said Mike.

For just one second the two drew themselves together preparatory to beginning the serious business of the interview, and in that second Psmith, turning from the glass, stepped between them.

"Get out of the light, Smith," said Mike.

Psmith waved him back with a deprecating gesture.

"My dear young friends," he said placidly, "if you *will* let your angry passions rise, against the direct advice of Doctor Watts, I suppose you must. But when you propose to claw each other in my study, in the midst of a hundred fragile and priceless ornaments, I lodge a protest. If you really feel that you want to scrap, for goodness' sake do it where there's some room. I don't want all the study furniture smashed. I know a bank whereon the wild thyme grows, only a few yards down the road, where you can scrap all night if you want to. How would it be to move on there? Any objections? None. Then shift ho! And let's get it over."

CHAPTER XXVI

CLEARING THE AIR

PSMITH was one of those people who lend a dignity to everything they touch. Under his auspices the most unpromising ventures became somehow enveloped in an atmosphere of measured stateliness. On the present occasion, what would have been, without his guiding hand, a mere unscientific scramble, took on something of the impressive formality of the National Sporting Club.

"The rounds," he said, producing a watch, as they passed through a gate into a field a couple of hundred yards from the house gate, "will be of three minutes' duration, with a minute rest in between. A man who is down will have ten seconds in which to rise. Are you ready, Comrades Adair and Jackson? Very well, then. Time."

After which, it was a pity that the actual fight did not quite live up to its referee's introduction. Dramatically, there should have been cautious sparring for openings and a number of tensely contested rounds, as if it had been the final of a boxing competition. But school fights, when they do occur—which is only once in a decade nowadays, unless you count junior school scuffles—are the outcome of weeks of suppressed bad blood, and are consequently brief and furious. In a boxing competition, however much one may want to win, one does not dislike one's opponent. Up to the moment when "time" was called, one was probably warmly attached to him, and at the end of the last round one expects to resume that attitude of mind. In a fight each party, as a rule, hates the other.

So it happened that there was nothing formal or cautious about the present battle. All Adair wanted was to get at

Mike, and all Mike wanted was to get at Adair. Directly Psmith called "time," they rushed together as if they meant to end the thing in half a minute.

It was this that saved Mike. In an ordinary contest with the gloves, with his opponent cool and boxing in his true form, he could not have lasted three rounds against Adair. The latter was a clever boxer, while Mike had never had a lesson in his life. If Adair had kept away and used his head, nothing could have prevented him winning.

As it was, however, he threw away his advantages, much as Tom Brown did at the beginning of his fight with Slogger Williams, and the result was the same as on that historic occasion. Mike had the greater strength, and, thirty seconds from the start, knocked his man clean off his feet with an unscientific but powerful right-hander.

This finished Adair's chances. He rose full of fight, but with all the science knocked out of him. He went in at Mike with both hands. The Irish blood in him, which for the ordinary events of life made him merely energetic and dashing, now rendered him reckless. He abandoned all attempt at guarding. It was the Frontal Attack in its most futile form, and as unsuccessful as a frontal attack is apt to be. There was a swift exchange of blows, in the course of which Mike's left elbow, coming into contact with his opponent's right fist, got a shock which kept it tingling for the rest of the day; and then Adair went down in a heap.

He got up slowly and with difficulty. For a moment he stood blinking vaguely. Then he lurched forward at Mike.

In the excitement of a fight—which is, after all, about the most exciting thing that ever happens to one in the course of one's life—it is difficult for the fighters to see what the spectators see. Where the spectators see an assault on an already beaten man, the fighter himself only sees a legitimate piece of self-defence against an opponent whose chances are equal to his own. Psmith saw, as anybody looking on would have seen, that Adair was done. Mike's blow had taken him within a fraction of an inch of the point of the jaw, and he was all but knocked out. Mike could not see this. All he understood was that his man was on his feet again and coming at him, so he hit out with all his strength; and this time Adair went down and stayed down.

"Brief," said Psmith, coming forward, "but exciting. We may take that, I think, to be the conclusion of the entertainment. I will now have a dash at picking up the slain. I shouldn't stop, if I were you. He'll be sitting up and taking notice soon, and if he sees you he may want to go on with the combat, which would do him no earthly good. If it's going to be continued in our next, there had better be a bit of an interval for alterations and repairs first."

"Is he hurt much, do you think?" asked Mike. He had seen knock-outs before in the ring, but this was the first time he had ever effected one on his own account, and Adair looked unpleasantly corpse-like.

"*He's* all right," said Psmith. "In a minute or two he'll be skipping about like a little lambkin. I'll look after him. You go away and pick flowers."

Mike put on his coat and walked back to the house. He was conscious of a perplexing whirl of new and strange emotions, chief among which was a curious feeling that he rather liked Adair. He found himself thinking that Adair was a good chap, that there was something to be said for his point of view, and that it was a pity he had knocked him about so much. At the same time, he felt an undeniable thrill of pride at having beaten him. The feat presented that interesting person, Mike Jackson, to him in a fresh and pleasing light, as one who had had a tough job to face and had carried it through. Jackson, the cricketer, he knew, but Jackson, the deliverer of knock-out blows, was strange to him, and he found this new acquaintance a man to be respected.

The fight, in fact, had the result which most fights have, if they are fought fairly and until one side has had enough. It revolutionized Mike's view of things. It shook him up, and drained the bad blood out of him. Where, before, he had seemed to himself to be acting with massive dignity, he now saw that he had simply been sulking like some wretched kid. There had appeared to him something rather fine in his policy of refusing to identify himself in any way with Sedleigh, a touch of the stone-walls-do-not-a-prison-make sort of thing. He now saw that his attitude was to be summed up in the words, "Sha'n't play."

It came upon Mike with painful clearness that he had been making an ass of himself.

He had come to this conclusion, after much earnest thought, when Psmith entered the study.

"How's Adair?" asked Mike.

"Sitting up and taking nourishment once more. We have been chatting. He's not a bad cove."

"He's all right," said Mike.

There was a pause. Psmith straightened his tie.

"Look here," he said, "I seldom interfere in terrestrial strife, but it seems to me that there's an opening here for a capable peace-maker, not afraid of work, and willing to give his services in exchange for a comfortable home. Comrade Adair's rather a stoutish fellow in his way. I'm not much on the 'Play up for the old school, Jones,' game, but everyone to his taste. I shouldn't have thought any-body would get overwhelmingly attached to this abode of wrath, but Comrade Adair seems to have done it. He's all for giving Sedleigh a much-needed boost-up. It's not a bad idea in its way. I don't see why one shouldn't humour him. Apparently he's been sweating since early childhood to buck the school up. And as he's leaving at the end of the term, it mightn't be a scaly scheme to give him a bit of a send-off, if possible, by making the cricket season a bit of a banger. As a start, why not drop him a line to say that you'll play against the M.C.C. tomorrow?"

Mike did not reply at once. He was feeling better dis-posed towards Adair and Sedleigh than he had felt, but he was not sure that he was quite prepared to go as far as a complete climb-down.

"It wouldn't be a bad idea," continued Psmith. "There's nothing like giving in to a man a bit every now and then.

It broadens the soul and improves the action of the skin. What seems to have fed up Comrade Adair, to a certain extent, is that Stone apparently led him to understand that you had offered to give him and Robinson places in your village team. You didn't, of course?"

"Of course not," said Mike indignantly.

"I told him he didn't know the old *noblesse oblige* spirit of the Jacksons. I said that you would scorn to tarnish the Jackson escutcheon by not playing the game. My eloquence convinced him. However, to return to the point under discussion, why not?"

"I don't—— What I mean to say——" began Mike.

"If your trouble is," said Psmith, "that you fear that you may be in unworthy company——"

"Don't be an ass."

"——Dismiss it. *I* am playing."

Mike stared.

"You're *what*? *You*?"

"I," said Psmith, breathing on a coat-button, and polishing it with his handkerchief.

"Can you play cricket?"

"You have discovered," said Psmith, "my secret sorrow."

"You're rotting."

"You wrong me, Comrade Jackson."

"Then why haven't you played?"

"Why haven't you?"

"Why didn't you come and play for Lower Borlock, I mean?"

"The last time I played in a village cricket match I was caught at point by a man in braces. It would have been madness to risk another such shock to my system. My nerves are so exquisitely balanced that a thing of that sort takes years off my life."

"No, but look here, Smith, bar rotting. Are you really any good at cricket?"

"Competent judges at Eton gave me to understand so. I was told that this year I should be a certainty for Lord's.

But when the cricket season came, where was I? Gone. Gone like some beautiful flower that withers in the night."

"But you told me you didn't like cricket. You said you only liked watching it."

"Quite right. I do. But at schools where cricket is compulsory you have to overcome your private prejudices. And in time the thing becomes a habit. Imagine my feelings when I found that I was degenerating, little by little, into a slow left-hand bowler with a swerve. I fought against it, but it was useless, and after a while I gave up the struggle, and drifted with the stream. Last year in a house match"—Psmith's voice took on a deeper tone of melancholy—"I took seven for thirteen in the second innings on a hard wicket. I did think, when I came here, that I had found a haven of rest, but it was not to be. I turn out to-morrow. What Comrade Outwood will say, when he finds that his keenest archæological disciple has deserted, I hate to think. However——"

Mike felt as if a young and powerful earthquake had passed. The whole face of his world had undergone a quick change. Here was he, the recalcitrant, wavering on the point of playing for the school, and here was Psmith, the last person whom he would have expected to be a player, stating calmly that he had been in the running for a place in the Eton eleven.

Then in a flash Mike understood. He was not by nature intuitive, but he read Psmith's mind now. Since the term began, he and Psmith had been acting on precisely similar motives. Just as he had been disappointed of the captaincy of cricket at Wrykyn, so had Psmith been disappointed of his place in the Eton team at Lord's. And they had both worked it off, each in his own way—Mike sullenly, Psmith whimsically, according to their respective natures—on Sedleigh.

If Psmith, therefore, did not consider it too much of a climb-down to renounce his resolution not to play for Sedleigh, there was nothing to stop Mike doing so, as—at the bottom of his heart—he wanted to do.

"By Jove," he said, "if you're playing, I'll play. I'll write a note to Adair now. But, I say"—he stopped— "I'm hanged if I'm going to turn out and field before breakfast tomorrow."

"That's all right. You won't have to. Adair won't be there himself. He's not playing against the M.C.C. He's sprained his wrist."

CHAPTER XXVII

IN WHICH PEACE IS DECLARED

"SPRAINED his wrist?" said Mike. "How did he do that?"

"During the brawl. Apparently one of his efforts got home on your elbow instead of your expressive countenance, and whether it was that your elbow was particularly tough or his wrist particularly fragile, I don't know. Anyhow, it went. It's nothing bad, but it'll keep him out of the game tomorrow."

"I say, what beastly rough luck! I'd no idea. I'll go round."

"Not a bad scheme. Close the door gently after you, and if you see anybody downstairs who looks as if he were likely to be going over to the shop, ask him to get me a small pot of some rare old jam and tell the man to chalk it up to me. The jam Comrade Outwood supplies to us at tea is all right, as a practical joke or as a food for those anxious to commit suicide, but useless to anybody who values life."

On arriving at Mr. Downing's and going to Adair's study, Mike found that his late antagonist was out. He left a note informing him of his willingness to play in the morrow's match. The lock-up bell rang as he went out of the house.

A spot of rain fell on his hand. A moment later there was a continuous patter, as the storm, which had been gathering all day, broke in earnest. Mike turned up his coat-collar, and ran back to Outwood's. "At this rate," he said to himself, "there won't be a match at all tomorrow."

When the weather decides, after behaving well for some weeks, to show what it can do in another direction, it does the thing thoroughly. When Mike woke the next morning the world was grey and dripping. Leaden-coloured clouds drifted over the sky, till there was not a trace of blue to be seen, and then the rain began again, in the gentle, determined way rain has when it means to make a day of it.

It was one of those bad days when one sits in the pavilion, damp and depressed, while figures in mackintoshes, with discoloured buckskin boots, crawl miserably about the field in couples.

Mike, shuffling across to school in a Burberry, met Adair at Downing's gate.

These moments are always difficult. Mike stopped—he could hardly walk on as if nothing had happened—and looked down at his feet.

"Coming across?" he said awkwardly.

"Right ho!" said Adair.

They walked on in silence.

"It's only about ten to, isn't it?" said Mike.

Adair fished out his watch, and examined it with an elaborate care born of nervousness.

"About nine to."

"Good. We've got plenty of time."

"Yes."

"I hate having to hurry over to school."

"So do I."

"I often do cut it rather fine, though."

"Yes. So do I."

"Beastly nuisance when one does."

"Beastly."

"It's only about a couple of minutes from the houses to the school, I should think, shouldn't you?"

"Not much more. Might be three."

"Yes. Three if one didn't hurry."

Another silence.

"Beastly day," said Adair.

"Rotten."

Silence again.

"I say," said Mike, scowling at his toes, "awfully sorry about your wrist."

"Oh, that's all right. It was my fault."

"Does it hurt?"

"Oh, no, rather not, thanks."

"I'd no idea you'd crocked yourself."

"Oh, no, that's all right. It was only right at the end. You'd have smashed me anyhow."

"Oh, rot."

"I bet you anything you like you would."

"I bet you I shouldn't. . . . Jolly hard luck, just before the match."

"Oh, no. . . . I say, thanks awfully for saying you'd play."

"Oh, rot. . . . Do you think we shall get a game?"

Adair inspected the sky carefully.

"I don't know. It looks pretty bad, doesn't it?"

"Rotten. I say, how long will your wrist keep you out of cricket?"

"Be all right in a week. Less, probably."

"Good."

"Now that you and Smith are going to play, we ought to have a jolly good season."

"Rummy, Smith turning out to be a cricketer."

"Yes. I should think he'd be a hot bowler, with his height."

"He must be jolly good if he was only just out of the Eton team last year."

"Yes."

"What's the time?" asked Mike.

Adair produced his watch once more.

"Five to."

"We've heaps of time."

"Yes, heaps."

"Let's stroll on a bit down the road, shall we?"

"Right ho!"

Mike cleared his throat.

"I say."

"Hullo?"

"I've been talking to Smith. He was telling me that you thought I'd promised to give Stone and Robinson places in the——"

"Oh, no, that's all right. It was only for a bit. Smith told me you couldn't have done, and I saw that I was an ass to think you could have. It was Stone seeming so dead certain that he could play for Lower Borlock if I chucked him from the school team that gave me the idea."

"He never even asked me to get him a place."

"No, I know."

"Of course, I wouldn't have done it, even if he had."

"Of course not."

"I didn't want to play myself, but I wasn't going to do a rotten trick like getting other fellows away from the team."

"No, I know."

"It was rotten enough, really, not playing myself."

"Oh, no. Beastly rough luck having to leave Wrykyn just when you were going to be captain, and come to a small school like this."

The excitement of the past few days must have had a stimulating effect on Mike's mind—shaken it up, as it were, for now, for the second time in two days, he displayed quite a creditable amount of intuition. He might have been misled by Adair's apparently deprecatory attitude towards Sedleigh, and blundered into a denunciation of the place. Adair had said "a small school like this" in the sort of voice which might have led his hearer to think that he was expected to say, "Yes, rotten little hole, isn't it?" or words to that effect. Mike, fortunately, perceived that the words were used purely from politeness, on the Chinese principle. When a Chinaman wishes to pay a compliment, he does so by belittling himself and his belongings.

He eluded the pitfall.

"What rot!" he said. "Sedleigh's one of the most sporting schools I've ever come across. Everybody's as keen as blazes. So they ought to be, after the way you've sweated."

Adair shuffled awkwardly.

"I've always been fairly keen on the place," he said. "But I don't suppose I've done anything much."

"You've loosened one of my front teeth," said Mike, with a grin, "if that's any comfort to you."

"I couldn't eat anything except porridge this morning. My jaw still aches."

For the first time during the conversation their eyes met, and the humorous side of the thing struck them simultaneously. They began to laugh.

"What fools we must have looked?" said Adair.

"*You* were all right. I must have looked rotten. I've never had the gloves on in my life. I'm jolly glad no one saw us except Smith, who doesn't count. Hullo, there's the bell. We'd better be moving on. What about this match? Not much chance of it from the look of the sky at present."

"It might clear before eleven. You'd better get changed, anyhow, at the interval, and hang about in case."

"All right. It's better than doing Thucydides with Downing. We've got maths till the interval, so I don't see anything of him all day; which won't hurt me."

"He isn't a bad sort of chap, when you get to know him," said Adair.

"I can't have done, then. I don't know which I'd least soon be, Downing or a black-beetle, except that if one was Downing one could tread on the black-beetle. Dash this rain. I got about half a pint down my neck just then. We shan't get a game today, or anything like it. As you're crocked, I'm not sure that I care much. You've been sweating for years to get the match on, and it would be rather rot playing it without you."

"I don't know that so much. I wish we could play because I'm certain, with you and Smith, we'd walk into them. They probably aren't sending down much of a team, and really, now that you and Smith are turning out, we've got a jolly hot lot. There's quite decent batting all the way through, and the bowling isn't so bad. If only we could have given this M.C.C. lot a really good hammering,

167

it might have been easier to get some good fixtures for next season. You see, it's all right for a school like Wrykyn, but with a small place like this you simply can't get the best teams to give you a match till you've done something to show that you aren't absolute rotters at the game. As for the schools, they're worse. They'd simply laugh at you. You were cricket secretary at Wrykyn last year. What would you have done if you'd had a challenge from Sedleigh? You'd either have laughed till you were sick, or else had a fit at the mere idea of the thing."

Mike stopped.

"By Jove, you've struck about the brightest scheme on record. I never thought of it before. Let's get a match on with Wrykyn."

"What! They wouldn't play us."

"Yes, they would. At least, I'm pretty sure they would. I had a letter from Strachan, the captain, yesterday, saying that the Ripton match had had to be scratched owing to illness. So they've got a vacant date. Shall I try them? I'll write to Strachan tonight, if you like. And they aren't strong this year. We'll smash them. What do you say?"

Adair was as one who has seen a vision.

"By Jove," he said at last, "if we only could!"

CHAPTER XXVIII

MR. DOWNING MOVES

THE rain continued without a break all the morning. The two teams, after hanging about dismally, and whiling the time away with stump-cricket in the changing-rooms, lunched in the pavilion at one o'clock. After which the M.C.C. captain, approaching Adair, moved that this merry meeting be considered off and himself and his men permitted to catch the next train back to town. To which Adair, seeing that it was out of the question that there should be any cricket that afternoon, regretfully agreed, and the first Sedleigh *v.* M.C.C. match was accordingly scratched.

Mike and Psmith, wandering back to the house, were met by a damp junior from Downing's, with a message that Mr. Downing wished to see Mike as soon as he was changed.

"What's he want me for?" inquired Mike.

The messenger did not know. Mr. Downing, it seemed, had not confided in him. All he knew was that the house-master was in the house, and would be glad if Mike would step across.

"A nuisance," said Psmith, "this incessant demand for you. That's the worst of being popular. If he wants you to stop to tea, edge away. A meal on rather a sumptuous scale will be prepared in the study against your return."

Mike changed quickly, and went off, leaving Psmith, who was fond of simple pleasures in his spare time, earnestly occupied with a puzzle which had been scattered through the land by a weekly paper. The prize for a solution was one thousand pounds, and Psmith had already informed Mike with some minuteness of his plans for the disposition of this sum. Meanwhile, he worked at it both in and out of school, generally with abusive comments on its inventor.

He was still fiddling away at it when Mike returned.

Mike, though Psmith was at first too absorbed to notice it, was agitated.

"I don't wish to be in any way harsh," said Psmith, without looking up, "but the man who invented this thing was a blighter of the worst type. You come and have a shot. For the moment I am baffled. The whisper flies round the clubs, 'Psmith is baffled.'"

"The man's an absolute drivelling ass," said Mike warmly.

"Me, do you mean?"

"What on earth would be the point of my doing it?"

"You'd gather in a thousand of the best. Give you a nice start in life."

"I'm not talking about your rotten puzzle."

"What *are* you talking about?"

"That ass Downing. I believe he's off his nut."

"Then your chat with Comrade Downing was not of the old-College-chums-meeting-unexpectedly-after-years'-separation type? What has he been doing to you?"

"He's off his nut."

"I know. But what did he do? How did the brainstorm burst? Did he jump at you from behind a door and bite a piece out of your leg, or did he say he was a tea-pot?"

Mike sat down.

"You remember that painting Sammy business?"

"As if it were yesterday," said Psmith. "Which it was, pretty nearly."

"He thinks I did it."

"Why? Have you ever shown any talent in the painting line?"

"The silly ass wanted me to confess that I'd done it. He as good as asked me to. Jawed a lot of rot about my finding it to my advantage later on if I behaved sensibly."

"Then what are you worrying about? Don't you know that when a master wants you to do the confessing-act, it simply means that he hasn't enough evidence to start in on you with? You're all right. The thing's a stand-off."

"Evidence!" said Mike. "My dear man, he's got enough evidence to sink a ship. He's absolutely sweating evidence at every pore. As far as I can see, he's been crawling about, doing the Sherlock Holmes business for all he's worth ever since the thing happened, and now he's dead certain that I painted Sammy."

"*Did* you, by the way?" said Psmith.

"No," said Mike shortly, "I didn't. But after listening to Downing I almost began to wonder if I hadn't. The man's got stacks of evidence to prove that I did."

"Such as what?"

"It's mostly about my shoes. But, dash it, you know all about that. Why, you were with him when he came and looked for them."

"It is true," said Psmith, "that Comrade Downing and I spent a very pleasant half-hour together inspecting shoes, but how does he drag you into it?"

"He swears one of the shoes was splashed with paint."

"Yes. He babbled to some extent on that point when I was entertaining him. But what makes him think that the shoe, if any, was yours?"

"He's certain that somebody in this house got one of his shoes splashed, and is hiding it somewhere. And I'm the only chap in the house who hasn't got a pair of shoes to show, so he thinks it's me. I don't know where the dickens my other shoe has gone. Edmund swears he hasn't seen it, and it's nowhere about. Of course I've got two pairs, but one's being soled. So I had to go over to school yesterday in gym shoes. That's how he spotted me."

Psmith sighed.

"Comrade Jackson," he said mournfully, "all this very sad affair shows the folly of acting from the best motives. In my simple zeal, meaning to save you unpleasantness, I have landed you, with a dull, sickening thud, right in the cart. Are you particular about dirtying your hands? If you aren't, just reach up that chimney a bit!"

Mike stared.

"What the dickens are you talking about?"

"Go on. Get it over. Be a man, and reach up the chimney."

"I don't know what the game is," said Mike, kneeling beside the fender and groping, "but—*Hullo*!"

"Ah ha!" said Psmith moodily.

Mike dropped the soot-covered object in the fender, and glared at it.

"It's my shoe!" he said at last.

"It *is*," said Psmith, "your shoe. And what is that red stain across the toe? Is it blood? No, 'tis not blood. It is red paint."

Mike seemed unable to remove his eyes from the shoe.

"How on earth did—— By Jove! I remember now. I kicked up against something in the dark when I was putting my bicycle back that night. It must have been the paint-pot."

"Then you were out that night?"

"Rather. That's what makes it so jolly awkward. It's too long to tell you now——"

"Your stories are never too long for me," said Psmith. Say on!"

"Well, it was like this." And Mike related the events which had led up to his midnight excursion. Psmith listened attentively.

"This," he said, when Mike had finished, "confirms my frequently stated opinion that Comrade Jellicoe is one of Nature's blitherers. So that's why he touched us for our hard-earned, was it?"

"Yes. Of course there was no need for him to have the money at all."

"And the result is that you are in something of a tight place. You're *absolutely* certain you didn't paint that dog? Didn't do it, by any chance, in a moment of absent-mindedness, and forgot all about it? No? No, I suppose not. I wonder who did!"

"It's beastly awkward. You see, Downing chased me

that night. That was why I rang the alarm bell. So, you see, he's certain to think that the chap he chased, which was me, and the chap who painted Sammy, are the same. I shall get landed both ways."

Psmith pondered.

"It *is* a tightish place," he admitted.

"I wonder if we could get this shoe clean," said Mike, inspecting it with disfavour.

"Not for a pretty considerable time."

"I suppose not. I say, I *am* in the cart. If I can't produce this shoe, they're bound to guess why."

"What exactly," asked Psmith, "was the position of affairs between you and Comrade Downing when you left him? Had you definitely parted brass-rags? Or did you simply sort of drift apart with mutual courtesies?"

"Oh, he said I was ill-advised to continue that attitude, or some rot, and I said I didn't care, I hadn't painted his bally dog, and he said very well, then, he must take steps, and—well, that was about all."

"Sufficient, too," said Psmith, "quite sufficient, I take it, then, that he is now on the war-path, collecting a gang, so to speak."

"I suppose he's gone to the Old Man about it."

"Probably. A very worrying time our headmaster is having, taking it all round, in connection with this painful affair. What do you think his move will be?"

"I suppose he'll send for me, and try to get something out of me."

"*He'll* want you to confess, too. Masters are all whales on confession. The worst of it is, you can't prove an alibi, because at about the time the foul act was perpetrated, you were playing Round-and-round-the-mulberry-bush with Comrade Downing. This needs thought. You had better put the case in my hands, and go out and watch the dandelions growing. I will think over the matter."

"Well, I hope you'll be able to think of something. I can't."

"Possibly. You never know."

There was a tap at the door.

"See how we have trained them," said Psmith. "They now knock before entering. There was a time when they would have tried to smash in a panel. Come in."

A small boy, carrying a straw hat adorned with the School House ribbon, answered the invitation.

"Oh, I say, Jackson," he said, "the headmaster sent me over to tell you he wants to see you."

"I told you so," said Mike to Psmith.

"Don't go," suggested Psmith. "Tell him to write."

Mike got up.

"All this is very trying," said Psmith. "I'm seeing nothing of you today." He turned to the small boy. "Tell Willie," he added, "that Mr. Jackson will be with him in a moment."

The emissary departed.

"*You're* all right," said Psmith encouragingly. "Just you keep on saying you're all right. Stout denial is the thing. Don't go in for any airy explanations. Simply stick to stout denial. You can't beat it."

With which expert advice, he allowed Mike to go on his way.

He had not been gone two minutes, when Psmith, who had leaned back in his chair, rapt in thought, heaved himself up again. He stood for a moment straightening his tie at the looking-glass; then he picked up his hat and moved slowly out of the door and down the passage. Thence, at the same dignified rate of progress, out of the house and in at Downing's front gate.

The postman was at the door when he got there, apparently absorbed in conversation with the parlour-maid. Psmith stood by politely till the postman, who had just been told it was like his impudence, caught sight of him, and, having handed over the letters in an ultra-formal and professional manner, passed away.

"Is Mr. Downing at home?" inquired Psmith.

He was, it seemed. Psmith was shown into the dining-room on the left of the hall, and requested to wait. He was examining a portrait of Mr. Downing which hung on the wall, when the house-master came in.

"An excellent likeness, sir," said Psmith, with a gesture of the hand towards the painting.

"Well, Smith," said Mr. Downing shortly, "what do you wish to see me about?"

"It was in connection with the regrettable painting of your dog, sir."

"Ha!" said Mr. Downing.

"I did it, sir," said Psmith, stopping and flicking a piece of fluff off his knee.

CHAPTER XXIX

THE ARTIST CLAIMS HIS WORK

THE line of action which Psmith had called Stout Denial is an excellent line to adopt, especially if you really are innocent, but it does not lead to anything in the shape of a bright and snappy dialogue between accuser and accused. Both Mike and the headmaster were oppressed by a feeling that the situation was difficult. The atmosphere was heavy, and conversation showed a tendency to flag. The headmaster had opened brightly enough, with a summary of the evidence which Mr. Downing had laid before him, but after that a massive silence had been the order of the day. There is nothing in this world quite so stolid and uncommunicative as a boy who has made up his mind to be stolid and uncommunicative; and the headmaster, as he sat and looked at Mike, who sat and looked past him at the bookshelves, felt awkward. It was a scene which needed either a dramatic interruption or a neat exit speech. As it happened, what it got was the dramatic interruption.

The headmaster was just saying, "I do not think you fully realize, Jackson, the extent to which appearances——" —which was practically going back to the beginning and starting again—when there was a knock at the door. A voice without said, "Mr. Downing to see you, sir," and the chief witness for the prosecution burst in.

"I would not have interrupted you," said Mr. Downing, "but——"

Not at all, Mr. Downing. Is there anything I can——?"

"I have discovered—I have been informed—— In

short, it was not Jackson, who committed the—who painted my dog."

Mike and the headmaster both looked at the speaker. Mike with a feeling of relief—for Stout Denial, unsupported by any weighty evidence, is a wearing game to play—the headmaster with astonishment.

"Not Jackson?" said the headmaster.

"No. It was a boy in the same house. Smith."

Psmith! Mike was more than surprised. He could not believe it. There is nothing which affords so clear an index to a boy's character as the type of rag which he considers humorous. Between what is a rag and what is merely a rotten trick there is a very definite line drawn. Masters, as a rule, do not realize this, but boys nearly always do. Mike could not imagine Psmith doing a rotten thing like covering a house-master's dog with red paint, any more than he could imagine doing it himself. They had both been amused at the sight of Sammy after the operation, but anybody, except possibly the owner of the dog, would have thought it funny at first. After the first surprise, their feeling had been that it was a rotten thing to have done and beastly rough luck on the poor brute. It was a kid's trick. As for Psmith having done it, Mike simply did not believe it."

"Smith!" said the headmaster. "What makes you think that?"

"Simply this," said Mr. Downing, with calm triumph, "that the boy himself came to me a few moments ago and confessed."

Mike was conscious of a feeling of acute depression. It did not make him in the least degree jubilant, or even thankful, to know that he himself was cleared of the charge. All he could think of was that Psmith was done for. This was bound to mean the sack. If Psmith had painted Sammy it meant that Psmith had broken out of his house at night: and it was not likely that the rules about nocturnal wandering were less strict at Sedleigh than at any other school in the kingdom. Mike felt, if possible, worse than he had felt when Wyatt had been caught on a similar occasion. It seemed as if Fate had a special grudge against his best friends. He did not make friends very quickly or easily, though he had always had scores of acquaintances—and with Wyatt and Psmith he had found himself at home from the first moment he had met them.

He sat there, with a curious feeling of having swallowed a heavy weight, hardly listening to what Mr. Downing was saying. Mr. Downing was talking rapidly to the headmaster, who was nodding from time to time.

Mike took advantage of a pause to get up. "May I go, sir?" he said.

"Certainly, Jackson, certainly," said the Head. "Oh, and er—, if you are going back to your house, tell Smith that I should like to see him."

"Yes, sir."

He had reached the door, when again there was a knock. "Come in," said the headmaster.

It was Adair.

"Yes, Adair?"

Adair was breathing rather heavily, as if he had been running.

"It was about Sammy—Sampson, sir," he said, looking at Mr. Downing.

"Ah, we know—— Well, Adair, what did you wish to say?"

"It wasn't Jackson who did it, sir."

"No, no, Adair. So Mr. Downing——"

"It was Dunster, sir."

Terrific sensation! The headmaster gave a sort of strangled yelp of astonishment. Mr. Downing leaped in his chair. Mike's eyes opened to their fullest extent.

"Adair!"

There was almost a wail in the headmaster's voice. The situation had suddenly become too much for him. His brain was swimming. That Mike, despite the evidence against him, should be innocent, was curious, perhaps, but not particularly startling. But that Adair should inform

178

him, two minutes after Mr. Downing's announcement of Psmith's confession, that Psmith, too, was guiltless, and that the real criminal was Dunster—it was this that made him feel that somebody, in the words of an American author, had played a mean trick on him, and substituted for his brain a side-order of cauliflower. Why Dunster, of all people? Dunster, who, he remembered dizzily, had left the school at Christmas. And why, if Dunster had really painted the dog, had Psmith asserted that he himself was the culprit? Why—why anything? He concentrated his mind on Adair as the only person who could save him from impending brain-fever.

"Adair!"

"Yes, sir?"

"What—*what* do you mean?"

"It *was* Dunster, sir. I got a letter from him only five minutes ago, in which he said that he had painted Sammy—Sampson, the dog, sir, for a rag—for a joke, and that, as he didn't want anyone here to get into a row—be punished for it, I'd better tell Mr. Downing at once. I tried to find Mr. Downing, but he wasn't in the house. Then I met Smith outside the house, and he told me that Mr. Downing had gone over to see you, sir."

"Smith told you?" said Mr. Downing.

"Yes, sir."

"Did you say anything to him about your having received this letter from Dunster?"

"I gave him the letter to read, sir."

"And what was his attitude when he had read it?"

"He laughed, sir."

"*Laughed!*" Mr. Downing's voice was thunderous.

"Yes, sir. He rolled about."

Mr. Downing snorted.

"But Adair," said the headmaster, "I do not understand how this thing could have been done by Dunster. He has left the school."

"He was down here for the Old Sedleighans' match, sir. He stopped the night in the village."

"And that was the night the—it happened?"

"Yes, sir."

"I see. Well, I am glad to find that the blame cannot be attached to any boy in the school. I am sorry that it is even an Old Boy. It was a foolish, discreditable thing to have done, but it is not as bad as if any boy still at the school had broken out of his house at night to do it."

"The sergeant," said Mr. Downing, "told me that the boy he saw was attempting to enter Mr. Outwood's house."

"Another freak of Dunster's, I suppose," said the head-master. "I shall write to him."

"If it was really Dunster who painted my dog," said Mr. Downing, "I cannot understand the part played by Smith in this affair. If he did not do it, what possible motive could he have had for coming to me of his own accord and deliberately confessing?"

"To be sure," said the headmaster, pressing a bell. "It is certainly a thing that calls for explanation. Barlow," he said, as the butler appeared, "kindly go across to Mr. Outwood's house and inform Smith that I should like to see him."

"If you please, sir, Mr. Smith is waiting in the hall."

"In the hall!"

"Yes, sir. He arrived soon after Mr. Adair, sir, saying that he would wait, as you would probably wish to see him shortly."

"H'm. Ask him to step up, Barlow."

"Yes, sir."

There followed one of the tensest "stage waits" of Mike's experience. It was not long, but, while it lasted, the silence was quite solid. Nobody seemed to have anything to say, and there was not even a clock in the room to break the stillness with its ticking. A very faint drip-drip of rain could be heard outside the window.

Presently there was a sound of footsteps on the stairs. The door was opened.

"Mr. Smith, sir."

The Old Etonian entered as would the guest of the evening who is a few moments late for dinner. He was cheerful, but slightly deprecating. He gave the impression of one who, though sure of his welcome, feels that some slight apology is expected from him. He advanced into the room with a gentle half-smile which suggested good-will to all men.

"It is still raining," he observed. "You wished to see me, sir?"

"Sit down, Smith."

"Thank you, sir."

He dropped into a deep arm-chair (which both Adair and Mike had avoided in favour of less luxurious seats) with the confidential cosiness of a fashionable physician calling on a patient, between whom and himself time has broken down the barriers of restraint and formality.

Mr. Downing burst out, like a reservoir that has broken its banks.

"Smith."

Psmith turned his gaze politely in the house-master's direction.

"Smith, you came to me a quarter of an hour ago and told me that it was you who had painted my dog Sampson."

"Yes, sir."

"It was absolutely untrue?"

"I am afraid so, sir."

"But, Smith——" began the headmaster.

Psmith bent forward encouragingly.

"—This is a most extraordinary affair. Have you no explanation to offer? What induced you to do such a thing?"

Psmith sighed softly.

"The craze of notoriety, sir," he replied sadly. "The curse of the present age."

"What!" replied the headmaster.

"It is remarkable," proceeded Psmith placidly, with the impersonal touch of one lecturing on generalities, "how frequently, when a murder has been committed, one finds men confessing that they have done it when it is out of the

181

question that they should have committed it. It is one of the most interesting problems with which anthropologists are confronted. Human nature——"

The headmaster interrupted.

"Smith," he said, "I should like to see you alone for a moment. Mr. Downing, might I trouble——? Adair, Jackson."

He made a motion towards the door.

When he and Psmith were alone, there was silence. Psmith leaned back comfortably in his chair. The headmaster tapped nervously with his foot on the floor.

"Er—Smith."

"Sir?"

The headmaster seemed to have some difficulty in proceeding. He paused again. Then he went on.

"Er—Smith, I do not for a moment wish to pain you, but have you—er, do you remember ever having had, as a child, let us say, any—er—severe illness? Any—er—*mental* illness?"

"No, sir."

"There is no—forgive me if I am touching on a sad subject—there is no—none of your near relatives have ever suffered in the way I—er—have described?"

"There isn't a lunatic on the list, sir," said Psmith cheerfully.

"Of course, Smith, of course," said the headmaster hurriedly, "I did not mean to suggest—quite so, quite so. . . . You think, then, that you confessed to an act which you had not committed purely from some sudden impulse which you cannot explain?"

"Strictly between ourselves, sir——"

Privately, the headmaster found Psmith's man-to-man attitude somewhat disconcerting, but he said nothing.

"Well, Smith?"

"I should not like it to go any further, sir."

"I will certainly respect any confidence——"

"I don't want anybody to know, sir. This is strictly between ourselves."

"I think you are sometimes apt to forget, Smith, the proper relations existing between boy and—— Well, never mind that for the present. We can return to it later. For the moment, let me hear what you wish to say. I shall, of course, tell nobody, if you do not wish it."

"Well, it was like this, sir," said Psmith. "Jackson happened to tell me that you and Mr. Downing seemed to think he had painted Mr. Downing's dog, and there seemed some danger of his being expelled, so I thought it wouldn't be an unsound scheme if I were to go and say I had done it. That was the whole thing. Of course, Dunster writing created a certain amount of confusion."

There was a pause.

"It was a very wrong thing to do, Smith," said the headmaster, at last, "but . . . You are a curious boy, Smith. Good night."

He held out his hand.

"Good night, sir," said Psmith.

"Not a bad old sort," said Psmith meditatively to himself, as he walked downstairs. "By no means a bad old sort. I must drop in from time to time and cultivate him."

Mike and Adair were waiting for him outside the front door.

"Well?" said Mike.

"You *are* the limit," said Adair. "What's he done?"

"Nothing. We had a very pleasant chat, and then I tore myself away."

"Do you mean to say he's not going to do a thing?"

"Not a thing."

"Well, you're a marvel," said Adair.

Psmith thanked him courteously. They walked on towards the houses.

"By the way, Adair," said Mike, as the latter started to turn in at Downing's, "I'll write to Strachan tonight about that match."

"What's that?" asked Psmith.

"Jackson's going to try and get Wrykyn to give us a

game," said Adair. "They've got a vacant date. I hope the dickens they'll do it."

"Oh, I should think they're certain to," said Mike. "Good night."

"And give Comrade Downing, when you see him," said Psmith, "my very best love. It is men like him who make this Merrie England of ours what is is."

"I say, Psmith," said Mike suddenly, "what really made you tell Downing you'd done it?"

"The craving for——"

"Oh, chuck it. You aren't talking to the Old Man now. I believe it was simply to get me out of a jolly tight corner."

Psmith's expression was one of pain.

"My dear Comrade Jackson," said he, "you wrong me. You make me writhe. I'm surprised at you. I never thought to hear those words from Michael Jackson."

"Well, I believe you did, all the same," said Mike obstinately. "And it was jolly good of you, too."

Psmith moaned.

CHAPTER XXX

SEDLEIGH v. WRYKYN

THE Wrykyn match was three-parts over, and things going badly for Sedleigh. In a way one might have said that the game was over, and that Sedleigh had lost; for it was a one day match, and Wrykyn, who had led on the first innings, had only to play out time to make the game theirs.

Sedleigh were paying the penalty for allowing themselves to be influenced by nerves in the early part of the day. Nerves lose more school matches than good play ever won. There is a certain type of school batsman who is a gift to any bowler when he once lets his imagination run away with him. Sedleigh, with the exception of Adair, Psmith, and Mike, had entered upon this match in a state of the most azure funk. Ever since Mike had received Strachan's answer and Adair had announced on the notice-board that on Saturday, July the twentieth, Sedleigh would play Wrykyn, the team had been all on the jump. It was useless for Adair to tell them, as he did repeatedly, on Mike's authority, that Wrykyn were weak this season, and that on their present form Sedleigh ought to win easily. The team listened, but were not comforted. Wrykyn might be below their usual strength, but then Wrykyn cricket, as a rule, reached such a high standard that this probably meant little. However weak Wrykyn might be—for them—there was a very firm impression among the members of the Sedleigh first eleven that the other school was quite strong enough to knock the cover off *them*. Experience counts enormously in school matches. Sedleigh had never been proved. The teams they played were the sort of sides which the Wrykyn second eleven would play. Whereas Wrykyn, from time immemorial, had been beating Ripton teams and Free Foresters teams and M.C.C. teams packed with county men and sending men to Oxford and Cambridge who got their blues as freshmen.

Sedleigh had gone on to the field that morning a depressed side.

It was unfortunate that Adair had won the toss. He had had no choice but to take first innings. The weather had been bad for the last week, and the wicket was slow and treacherous. It was likely to get worse during the day, so Adair had chosen to bat first.

Taking into consideration the state of nerves the team was in, this in itself was a calamity. A school eleven are always at their worst and nerviest before lunch. Even on their own ground they find the surroundings lonely and unfamiliar. The sublety of the bowlers becomes magnified. Unless the first pair make a really good start, a collapse almost invariably ensues.

Today the start had been gruesome beyond words. Mike, the bulwark of the side, the man who had been brought up on Wrykyn bowling, and from whom, whatever might happen to the others, at least a fifty was expected— Mike, going in first with Barnes and taking first over, had played inside one from Bruce, the Wrykyn slow bowler, and had been caught at short slip off his second ball.

That put the finishing touch on the panic. Stone, Robinson, and the others, all quite decent punishing batsmen when their nerves allowed them to play their own game, crawled to the wickets, declined to hit out at anything, and were clean bowled, several of them, playing back to half-volleys. Adair did not suffer from panic, but his batting was not equal to his bowling, and he had fallen after hitting one four. Seven wickets were down for thirty when Psmith went in.

Psmith had always disclaimed any pretensions to batting skill, but he was undoubtedly the right man for a crisis like this. He had an enormous reach, and he used it. Three consecutive balls from Bruce he turned into full-tosses and swept to the leg-boundary, and, assisted by Barnes, who had been sitting on the splice in his usual manner, he raised the total to seventy-one before being yorked, with his score at thirty-five. Ten minutes later the innings was over, with Barnes not out sixteen, for seventy-nine.

Wrykyn had then gone in, lost Strachan for twenty before lunch, and finally completed their innings at a quarter to four for a hundred and thirty-one.

This was better than Sedleigh had expected. At least eight of the team had looked forward dismally to an afternoon's leather-hunting. But Adair and Psmith, helped by the wicket, had never been easy, especially Psmith, who had taken six wickets, his slows playing havoc with the tail.

It would be too much to say that Sedleigh had any hope of pulling the game out of the fire; but it was a comfort, they felt, at any rate, having another knock. As is usual at this stage of a match, their nervousness had vanished, and they felt capable of better things than in the first innings.

It was on Mike's suggestion that Psmith and himself went in first. Mike knew the limitations of the Wrykyn bowling, and he was convinced that, if they could knock Bruce off, it might be possible to rattle up a score sufficient to give them the game, always provided Wrykyn collapsed in the second innings. And it seemed to Mike that the wicket would be so bad then that they easily might.

So he and Psmith had gone in at four o'clock to hit. And they had hit. The deficit had been wiped off, all but a dozen runs, when Psmith was bowled, and by that time Mike was set and in his best vein. He treated all the bowlers alike. And when Stone came in, restored to his proper frame of mind, and lashed out stoutly, and after him Robinson and the rest, if looked as if Sedleigh had a chance again. The score was a hundred and twenty when Mike, who had just reached his fifty, skied one to Strachan at cover. The time was twenty-five past five.

As Mike reached the pavilion, Adair declared the innings closed.

Wrykyn started batting at twenty-five minutes to six,

with sixty-nine to make if they wished to make them, and an hour and ten minutes during which to keep up their wickets if they preferred to take things easy and go for a win on the first innings.

At first it looked as if they meant to knock off the runs, for Strachan forced the game from the first ball, which was Psmith's, and which he hit into the pavilion. But, at fifteen, Adair bowled him. And when, two runs later, Psmith got the next man stumped, and finished up his over with a c-and-b, Wrykyn decided that it was not good enough. Seventeen for three, with an hour all but five minutes to go, was getting too dangerous. So Drummond and Rigby, the next pair, proceeded to play with caution, and the collapse ceased.

This was the state of the game at the point at which this chapter opened. Seventeen for three had become twenty-four for three, and the hands of the clock stood at ten minutes past six. Changes of bowling had been tried, but there seemed no chance of getting past the batsmen's defence. They were playing all the good balls, and refused to hit at the bad.

A quarter past six struck, and then Psmith made a suggestion which altered the game completely.

"Why don't you have a shot this end?" he said to Adair, as they were crossing over. "There's a spot on the off which might help you a lot. You can break like blazes if only you land on it. It doesn't help my leg-breaks a bit, because they won't hit at them."

Barnes was on the point of beginning to bowl, when Adair took the ball from him. The captain of Outwood's retired to short leg with an air that suggested that he was glad to be relieved of his prominent post.

The next moment Drummond's off-stump was lying at an angle of forty-five. Adair was absolutely accurate as a bowler, and he had dropped his first ball right on the worn patch.

Two minutes later Drummond's successor was retiring to the pavilion, while the wicket-keeper straightened the stumps again.

There is nothing like a couple of unexpected wickets for altering the atmosphere of a game. Five minutes before, Sedleigh had been lethargic and without hope. Now there was a stir and buzz all round the ground. There were twenty-five minutes to go, and five wickets were down. Sedleigh was on top again.

The next man seemed to take an age coming out. As a matter of fact, he walked more rapidly than a batsman usually walks to the crease.

Adair's third ball dropped just short of the spot. The batsman, hitting out, was a shade too soon. The ball hummed through the air a couple of feet from the ground in the direction of mid-off, and Mike, diving to the right, got to it as he was falling, and chucked it up.

After that the thing was a walk-over. Psmith clean bowled a man in his next over; and the tail, demoralized by the sudden change in the game, collapsed uncompromisingly. Sedleigh won by thirty-five runs with eight minutes in hand.

Psmith and Mike sat in their study after lock-up, discussing things in general and the game in particular.

"I feel like a beastly renegade, playing against Wrykyn," said Mike. "Still, I'm glad we won. Adair's a jolly good sort, and it'll make him happy for weeks."

"When I last saw Comrade Adair," said Psmith, "he was going about in a sort of trance, beaming vaguely and wanting to stand people things at the shop."

"He bowled awfully well."

"Yes," said Psmith. "I say, I don't wish to cast a gloom over this joyful occasion in any way, but you say Wrykyn are going to give Sedleigh a fixture again next year?"

"Well?"

"Well, have you thought of the massacre which will ensue? You will have left, Adair will have left. Incidentally, I shall have left. Wrykyn will swamp them."

"I suppose they will. Still, the great thing, you see, is to get the thing started. That's what Adair was so keen on. Now Sedleigh has beaten Wrykyn, he's satisfied. They can get fixtures with decent clubs, and work up to playing the big schools. You've got to start somehow. So it's all right, you see."

"And, besides," said Psmith, reflectively, "in an emergency they can always get Comrade Downing to bowl for them, what? Let us now sally out and see if we can't promote a rag of some sort in this abode of wrath. Comrade Outwood has gone over to dinner at the School House, and it would be a pity to waste a somewhat golden opportunity. Shall we stagger?"

They staggered.

READ MORE IN PENGUIN

In every corner of the world, on every subject under the sun, Penguin represents quality and variety – the very best in publishing today.

For complete information about books available from Penguin – including Puffins, Penguin Classics and Arkana – and how to order them, write to us at the appropriate address below. Please note that for copyright reasons the selection of books varies from country to country.

In the United Kingdom: Please write to *Dept. EP, Penguin Books Ltd, Bath Road, Harmondsworth, West Drayton, Middlesex UB7 ODA*

In the United States: Please write to *Consumer Sales, Penguin Putnam Inc., P.O. Box 999, Dept. 17109, Bergenfield, New Jersey 07621-0120.* VISA and MasterCard holders call 1-800-253-6476 to order Penguin titles

In Canada: Please write to *Penguin Books Canada Ltd, 10 Alcorn Avenue, Suite 300, Toronto, Ontario M4V 3B2*

In Australia: Please write to *Penguin Books Australia Ltd, P.O. Box 257, Ringwood, Victoria 3134*

In New Zealand: Please write to *Penguin Books (NZ) Ltd, Private Bag 102902, North Shore Mail Centre, Auckland 10*

In India: Please write to *Penguin Books India Pvt Ltd, 210 Chiranjiv Tower, 43 Nehru Place, New Delhi 110 019*

In the Netherlands: Please write to *Penguin Books Netherlands bv, Postbus 3507, NL-1001 AH Amsterdam*

In Germany: Please write to *Penguin Books Deutschland GmbH, Metzlerstrasse 26, 60594 Frankfurt am Main*

In Spain: Please write to *Penguin Books S. A., Bravo Murillo 19, 1° B, 28015 Madrid*

In Italy: Please write to *Penguin Italia s.r.l., Via Benedetto Croce 2, 20094 Corsico, Milano*

In France: Please write to *Penguin France, Le Carré Wilson, 62 rue Benjamin Baillaud, 31500 Toulouse*

In Japan: Please write to *Penguin Books Japan Ltd, Kaneko Building, 2-3-25 Koraku, Bunkyo-Ku, Tokyo 112*

In South Africa: Please write to *Penguin Books South Africa (Pty) Ltd, Private Bag X14, Parkview, 2122 Johannesburg*